# THE SPIDER:
# THE MAYOR OF HELL

THE **MASTER** OF **MEN**!

# SPIDER®

# THE MAYOR OF HELL

*By Grant Stockbridge*

STEEGER BOOKS • 2020

PUBLISHING HISTORY

"The Mayor of Hell" originally appeared in the January 1936 (Vol. 7, No. 4) issue of
*The Spider* magazine. Copyright 2020 by Argosy Communications, Inc. All rights
reserved.

# CHAPTER 1
## THE SPIDER IS TRAPPED

RICHARD WENTWORTH had his violin tucked beneath his chin, his eyes half-closed. Music poured in a silver stream from the Stradivarius. His face was in utter repose, the firm, straight lips relaxed, the harsh lines which often gashed his cheeks now smoothed out. For once, he was off-guard....

The slight opening of the French doors which he faced was silent—as gradual as sleep. They moved by imperceptible stages. The black sky—the glow of New York's lights thrown upward toward the penthouse—became visible between them, nothing more. No hands of the person who moved them, no hint of a presence there....

Wentworth played on, bemused in the music he passionately loved. Why should even he, whom death stalked each hour of the day and night, fear anything here in his penthouse? The entire fifteen-story building was his, and he had erected multiple safeguards. It was true that enemies had invaded his sanctum before this, but... He played on, and the doors swung wider.

It was no sound, no movement, that finally roused him, but the coldness of the crisp fall night creeping in from those opened windows. It reached his forehead, his dextrous fingers... Most men would have looked up, startled, to find the source of the coldness—and would have died! Wentworth had lived as a comrade with sudden death, when a heartbeat of hesitation

1

would have spelled instantaneous extinction. He did not delay now. At the cold touch of the air, like the hand of death upon his forehead, Wentworth let go with every muscle in his body and collapsed to the floor.

In the same instant he sensed that the French doors had been

**Before this, Wentworth had never
tried to kill officers of the Law!**

swung wide. He saw a man leap into the room, and a sub-machine gun yammered its thunderous laughter of death. The lead screamed just over where Wentworth had fallen. Bullets chewed across the keys of the massive organ which filled one end of the music room, moved downward to sew a seam of death across Wentworth's chest.

Richard Wentworth felt utter amazement. It was not that he had never been so attacked before. He had thrown all his wealth, all his keen mentality and superb body into the battle against crime, and many attempts had been made on his life. Secretly, he was that cold killer of the night who, because of the tiny red seal which he affixed upon the foreheads of the slain—was called the Spider.

But few of the Underworld, though they hated his grim and deadly justice with an undying bitterness, had discovered the secret of his identity. And for six months there had been no outbreak of the Underworld which the police could not handle, no criminal genius had arisen to enlist the minions of crime in a murdering legion against humanity. Wentworth had been lulled into a sense of security. Tonight he had been relaxed, off-guard—unarmed.

**WENTWORTH'S LIPS** were thin and cold against his teeth. He felt the instantaneous hard thumping of his heart which comes to a man who knows death is damnably near. But he knew no fear. Even in the midst of his amazement at the stunning quickness of the attack, his swift mind raced to the only possible action which could save him. Wentworth's heart was torn at the thing he did, but there was no help for it and no hesitation. He whirled his priceless Stradivarius in a swift, short arc and sent it hurtling toward the face of the machine gunner!

The violin had little weight. But a man will dodge from a

feather flying straight at his eyes. The violin caught the dodging man on the right cheek and eye, blinded him for seconds. He did not cease firing. The muzzle of the Thompson gun poured out forty-five caliber bullets in a smoking stream. They swept wildly over the room, smashed a hanging crystal chandelier which was incalculably valuable, embroidered the bronze pipes of the organ, traced crazy patterns of holes across the polished floor.

Wentworth was on his feet as he hurled the violin. He lunged to one side, reached the grand piano at the man's right hand and went under. He was still without a weapon. The violin bow was a ridiculous sliver of wood, even though it was strongly braced.

As Wentworth reached the piano and ducked beneath it, the man recovered from the blow of the violin, smashed now on the floor. He stopped the chatter of his gun, swept the room with amazed eyes. It would not, could not, last, of course. He, or the men who undoubtedly accompanied him, would soon discover Wentworth beneath the piano. There could be no hesitation. Wentworth did not even check his lunge. Straight under, toward the legs of the machine gunner, then out in a crouching, head-first dive.

Wentworth's shoulder struck the man's right knee from the side, slammed him to the floor. The gun crashed down. Wentworth's arms released their hold instantly, and he was at the man's throat. Not strangling him; that was too slow. Two stiffened fingers struck savagely at nerve centers on the side of the throat, paralyzing the heart action, the lungs. The Tommy man went limp. Wentworth's eyes shot to the door. A man was standing there with an automatic in his hand. His eyes were strained wide. He was frightened, but his fear was the sort that kills—other people. The automatic hammered out lead.

Wentworth flopped to the cover of the unconscious man's body, felt it jerk as bullets plucked into it. His eyes slid desperately sideways. The sub-machine gun was out of reach, the futile violin bow had snapped in his hand when he dived. He clawed at the coat pocket of the man he had tackled. Lead burned a groove along his arms, numbed it with fiery pain. He whipped the fingers, tried again and found a gun in the man's pocket. No time to withdraw it. The second gunman was moving closer, hoarding his bullets, waiting until he could get a fair target. Wentworth twisted the gun inside the pocket, squeezed the trigger twice blindly, jerked his head up and fired again.

The third shot took the advancing gunman dead center in the forehead. The heavy lead punched him off his feet, spilled him dead upon the floor. Before his body had even struck, Wentworth had the automatic out of the pocket. With swift sureness, he shot out the three lights of the room, and rolled toward the protection of the wall….

EVEN AS he moved, bullets began to pound upon the floor and, from a hundred yards away, a machine gun—no Thompson this time, but a full-sized heavy weapon—stammered its coughing fury. Under cover of the wall, Wentworth rose to his feet, stood with the emptied automatic in his hand. He whistled out a long breath between his pursed lips, shook his head sharply, then sidled cautiously toward the arch which opened on the dimly lighted drawing room.

"Keep back," he shouted to his servants inside. "I'm all right."

He saw a shadow loom in the arch, a tall, turbaned figure. There was the glint of a knife in the hand. "Back, Ram Singh!" Wentworth ordered. "There are only dead men in here."

He stepped swiftly into the broad, long living room. A shaded lamp in the corner gave the only light and the terrace French doors, with their bulletproof glass, were closed. The Sikh to whom Wentworth had spoken, stepped back, sliding his knife into the scabbard at his sash. A broad-shouldered man in chauffeur's livery burst through the portiered door from the hall with a revolver in his hand. He slid to a stop as he saw Wentworth.

"What's up, sir?" he asked anxiously.

Wentworth shook his head. He was frowning, his gray-blue eyes puzzled, his lean, strong face somber. "Don't know, Jackson. Attempted assassination by unknown parties. I killed two men. Tell Jenkyns to phone Miss Nita the usual warning."

THE USUAL warning! How many times in the past, he or Jenkyns had telephoned Nita van Sloan that there was a new warfare—that once more the man she loved was plunging into the maelstrom of death and destruction, fighting the Underworld to save humanity from new peril! For when criminals attacked Wentworth in his own personality, they most often struck, too, at the one woman in the world who knew his secret, and whom he loved. Yes, she must be warned at once.

From its distant ambuscade, the machine gun battered again and frosting covered the bullet-proof glass of the French doors.

Wentworth's butler, formal old Jenkyns, came in at as fast a pace as he ever allowed himself. His ruddy face was paler. There was a slight disorder in his curly white hair.

"Oh, Master Dick," he gasped. "I tried to call the police—to call Miss Nita—but the wire is dead."

"Private phone, too?"

"Yes, Master Dick."

Wentworth's fine mobile lips moved in a slight, grim smile. "Then the attack is not over. *Ram Singh!*"

*"Han, sahib!"* The turbaned Sikh bowed, lifting his cupped hands to his forehead.

"Rifles. My automatics." Ram Singh *salaamed*, white teeth flashed amid his bushy beard as he went swiftly from the room. "Jenkyns, get a gun and guard the dumbwaiter. *Jackson!*"

The chauffeur saluted, eagerness glinting in his blue eyes. His wide muscular jaw was set. They had fought side by side in the world-war, Sergeant Jackson and Major Wentworth.

"Yes, Major?"

"The hall and doors are your charge. Ram Singh and I will take the terrace."

"Yes, Major!" Jackson pivoted, went marching to the hall.

Wentworth stood staring at the door. He looked down at the empty automatic he held. What in the name of heaven was behind this attack? It was fantastic—a battle with machine guns in the middle of Manhattan! He turned slowly as a pane of bulletproof glass fell from the door under the hammering of high-power bullets. A searchlight blazed out and bathed the terrace outside, the interior of the room with white light.

By the gods! Regardless of who was behind this attack, it was plain that it would be a battle to the death…!

## CHAPTER 2
## TO ARREST THE SPIDER

R AM SINGH entered on swift, soundless feet, his bearded face happy above the three rifles, the brace of automatics and the two long, sharp-edged swords he carried.

Wentworth laughed suddenly, stepped forward to take his automatics, forty-five caliber Colts with test barrels. He checked each, slid back the bolts to see that cartridges were in the chambers, examined the clips and thumbed on the safety. He thrust them into his waist-band, then took a rifle.

It was a new type of weapon, the sort that the United States army would use if it ever fought another war. Smaller caliber than the old Springfield, chambering ten cartridges of tremendous velocity, which it injected and ejected automatically. He examined that as he had the automatics, then he sank on one knee and leveled the rifle at the pane that had been shot out. The machine gun began to flicker blue and yellow flame on the apartment roof across the street. Wentworth squeezed the trigger. The gun stopped.

He rose to his feet with a quiet smile. "Shoot out the searchlight, Ram Singh," he said. "I'm going to search the two men I killed."

Before he reached the door of the music room, the searchlight was smashed to darkness by two quick shots from the drawing-room. Wentworth crouched low and moved over beside the two bodies. He hauled them rapidly to cover, began to go through their pockets. Of one thing he was sure. This attack upon him undoubtedly heralded some new Underworld leader's rise. Who he was or what he sought, there was no way of telling....

The bodies yielded no clue and Wentworth moved back to the drawing-room.

"Keep to cover," he instructed Ram Singh. "We have no reserves and it is not necessary for a warrior such as you to prove his bravery. If a machine gun fires, silence it. Put out any new searchlights."

Ram Singh's dark eyes held unswervingly on Wentworth's face. They were devoted eyes. They said clearly that this man would gladly lay down his life for his master.

Wentworth put on a dark hat, picked up one of the swords Ram Singh had brought and tried its balance. He took that in his left hand and went toward the door.

"I am going out on the terrace, Ram Singh," he explained. "That is our first line of defense."

Jackson glanced in from the hall and his eyes met those of Ram Singh. These two were completely serious, unsmiling, but there was a pledge in that gaze. Afterward, they looked toward the man they served.

Wentworth's shoulders were less broad than Jackson's, but they were in perfect proportion to his lithe height. His body was hard-boned, flat-muscled, there was strength and poise in every movement, and there was more than that. His shoulders had a confident set and there was a touch of arrogance in the poise of his well-shaped head. Here was a man born to command.

AT THE French doors, Wentworth paused, seeming to feel their combined stare. He turned about and gave them a slow, grave smile, then he faced about and strode out into the darkness…. At first, the night shrouded everything, but presently, he could make out the low bulwark that surrounded the terrace, the white glisten of chairs and an umbrella table, the dark masses of shrubs. On the right and ahead of him, the railing of the terrace faced fifteen stories of empty space. To his left, there was a small section of roof through which the housing of the elevator and dumbwaiter shafts thrust.

In the chasm of darkness that was Fifth Avenue, police sirens were wailing. The machine gun began to stammer again and Ram Singh's rifle spoke three times before it was silent. The rhythm of an airplane motor pulled Wentworth's stare upward. There were no lights, but the plane was close, he knew, and drawing nearer. The motor cut and he could hear the whistle of wind against wires and struts….

Wentworth's mouth jerked open in a silent cry. He knew without any question what was to come. He lifted his automatics, dropping the sword with a silvery ring, but there was still no target. Abruptly, twin bunches of orange flame burst out of the darkness and machine gun bullets hammered across the floor of the terrace.

Wentworth flung flat against the base of the wall. A rifle blasted upward from the French doors of the music-room, emptied itself. A deadly rain of machine gun bullets thudded along the wall of the penthouse, shivered the French doors. Without even a preliminary glimpse of a falling bomb, the night was split wide open with scarlet-and-white flame.

Half-stunned, Wentworth scrambled to his feet and dashed for the house. His eyes were dazzled with light and the machine gun opened up again. He stumbled over debris and came down on hands and knees. He found himself gazing into a hole which revealed the apartment below his own.

Slowly, he circled it and entered the house. He realized that the airplane was swinging about again, that lead was whispering through rooms no longer protected by bullet-proof glass. Wentworth found Ram Singh binding up his left arm.

"*Wah!* It is nothing," Ram Singh scoffed. "A bit of glass from a broken window…."

His voice was drowned in the crash of a second bomb. The end wall of the penthouse trembled and collapsed into the apartment below. Wentworth hurried Ram Singh behind the protection of the hall wall. Machine-gun bullets hammered the wall, tore still hanging portieres in the doorway to shreds. Jackson stood motionless at his loophole, watching the outer hallway.

"Suggest retreat, Major," he said, without expression. "We can join the police downstairs. *Alerte,*" he broke off sharply. "Elevator coming up, sir!"

WENTWORTH SPRANG to another loophole, watched the elevator indicator swing slowly around a semi-circle of numbers. He was frowning. Enemies, or police? Either way, he was ready. The elevator stopped, and Wentworth set his automatic's muzzle to the loophole. The door slid back, and… three

men in police uniform stepped
out, followed by another in civilian garb. Daniel Fogarty, deputy
commissioner. Wentworth knew
him, but he did not open the door.
He spoke into an annunciator
which repeated his words in the
hall.

"THE MAYOR
OF HELL"

"What is it, Fogarty?" he said.

Fogarty spun about, small eyes
questing for the source of the voice, but the loud-speaker was
hidden in an alabaster vase.

"Wentworth?" Fogarty asked hesitantly.

"Wentworth speaking."

"Richard Wentworth," Fogarty's voice became heavy, solemn,
"I have a warrant for your arrest."

Wentworth frowned, his blue-gray eyes tightening. "Would
it be impudent," he said drily, "to ask the charge?"

Fogarty drew himself up. His face was pale, and it was obvious this speech from a hidden source worried him. He cleared
his throat. "Murder, Mr. Wentworth, is the charge."

"What murder?" Wentworth demanded harshly. "What are
you talking about?"

There was a greenish cast to Fogarty's face. "A lot of murders,"
he roared hoarsely. "You're charged with being the Spider!"

WENTWORTH'S LIPS twisted wryly. It had been many
months, years in fact, since anyone had dared to bring that

13

charge against Richard Wentworth. It was rather curious that it came co-incidentally with this murderous attack.

"If you will ask Commissioner Flynn to come up and deliver the warrant," Wentworth said shortly, "I will surrender."

Fogarty's head wobbled from side to side. "Flynn's dead," he gulped. "Bomb from an airplane got him."

Wentworth straightened away from the wall, away from the loophole and stared at the plaster before him with wide, unseeing eyes. So Flynn was dead! His companion through many a perilous night, an upright man, a soldier... Wentworth's fists knotted stonily at his sides. "You'll have to defer the arrest, Fogarty," he said stiffly. "For the present, it would seem I'm safer from death here than in your hands."

The blood rushed back into Fogarty's face, made it dark with anger. "You'll come out at once," he thundered, "or we'll come in and get you."

Wentworth laughed shortly. "Help yourself." He turned away from the loophole. The machine gun was hammering outside, the thud of bullets tattooed along the wall. Ram Singh, kneeling by the door, fired with slow deliberation back through the

RICHARD WENTWORTH

drawing-room. Suspicion crowded Wentworth's mind. It was ridiculous of Fogarty, coming to serve his warrant in the midst of this attack. Either that, or… or Fogarty was allied with the killers! A bomb burst somewhere near and the walls quivered.

Wentworth's eyes narrowed in sudden anger. He whirled back to the loophole. Fogarty was shouting, urging his men to the attack.

A policeman stepped up to the main door of Wentworth's apartment and fired at the lock. The bullet ricocheted from steel and bit into the man's leg, spilled him to the floor.

"They've shot down an officer!" Fogarty roared. "Kill them. Don't take them alive."

Wentworth's gun came up slowly to the loophole, his lips thinning back from his teeth. He didn't make war on the police, but it seemed that Deputy Commissioner Fogarty had forgotten that he served the city, that he had thrown in with criminals. He had seen as plainly as Wentworth that the bullet that had felled the officer had not come from within, yet he was crying out that Wentworth be killed without mercy. Yes, he was an ally of the criminals. There was no longer any doubt, but it would be madness to shoot now. Wentworth cut off the annunciator.

"Do you want to join the police now, Jackson?" he asked harshly.

Jackson's lips were as hard, as solid-looking as Wentworth's own. "Shall I shoot him?" he asked hoarsely. "Or will you?"

Wentworth shook his head. "Neither of us. They could prove that murder."

Ram Singh was at his elbow, offering one of the keen swords. *"Sahib,"* he whispered. "Five have crossed the terrace railing and are hidden where bullets cannot reach them. It is time for my master to go."

## CHAPTER 3
## FUGITIVE

WENTWORTH STARED down at the sword in Ram Singh's hand, reached out slowly and took its hilt. Time for the Spider to flee, if he expected to survive this night.

Wentworth laughed harshly. "Not yet, Ram Singh. First, we shall give them a little lesson."

He thrust the sword through the corner of his coat, palmed his automatics and moved soft-footed along the corridor toward the servant's wing. It overlooked the section of the roof that was not a terrace.

"Narcotic gas, Jackson," he said shortly as he passed the chauffeur. "If any more police come, gas them, too."

Ram Singh moved with him, hand on the hilt of his knife. He could use firearms superbly, but his master carried guns. A knife was more to his own liking. His teeth showed white through his beard: *Wah!* But this would be a slaying!

Wentworth led the way through darkness that was diminished only by the sky-glow outside. He entered an unused servants' bedroom that gave on the roof. Two men crouched outside a window, silhouetted against the brighter darkness of the sky. This window was bullet-proof, too.

They would not open it readily—unless Wentworth helped them.

"Is thy knife ready, my warrior?" he whispered, using the Punjabi which was native to Ram Singh.

Ram Singh's knife whispered harshly against its sheath and

17

its steel gleamed. Together, on opposite sides of the window, they moved toward the men. Wentworth had thrust his automatics into his belt in favor of the sword. If they could eliminate these men silently.... Each on a side of the window, Wentworth and Ram Singh laid the hand that did not hold a weapon upon the sash, hiding their bodies behind the wall. At a signal, a hiss from Wentworth, they flung the window up.

The two men outside were crouched, using tools on the window. Their hands were empty of weapons, but even if they had been ready, it would not have availed them. Wentworth's sword was a streak of light. Ram Singh's knife was no slower— and men with severed windpipes can make no sound. Their threshing death agony was drowned in the never-slacking hammer of the machine gun.

Wentworth was first through the window. He switched his sword to his left hand. "Ram Singh, they must be coming up the dumbwaiter shafts. Stop them."

Ram Singh lifted his knife to his forehead and became a drifting shadow. Wentworth moved toward the balustrade which surrounded his terrace. As he advanced, he heard a revolver roar out in rapid fire, its hollow note proving that it was within the penthouse. The devil! Was he too late? He reached the balustrade in a half-dozen lunging strides, peered above it with his automatic ready. Instantly, he began to shoot. Nothing hurried or wild about his firing. Lead sped as deliberately—and as accurately—as on a target range.

There were seven men charging toward the drawing-room, leaping over the debris of its collapsed wall. One crumpled before Wentworth fired. The attackers were caught in the bitter cross-fire, of Jackson's and Wentworth's guns. On the fifth shot, Wentworth ceased. The seven were down….

SWORD IN hand, Wentworth hand-vaulted the balustrade, and crouching low, moved across the debris-littered terrace. If one of the men was still alive, it might be possible to learn something of what lay behind all this. Wentworth caught movement, a glint of steel. He dropped to a knee and a bullet swished past his head. His automatic spat and the man who had fired groaned. Wentworth reached him in a single leap, snatched the gun away from the reach of his left hand. His bullet had smashed the right beyond any possible danger….

Glittering hatred shone from the man's eyes and a stream of unutterable abuse poured from his mouth. Wentworth put the sword point against the man's throat.

"I don't care for your accent, my man," Wentworth said lightly. "It grates upon the ear."

The cursing stopped in a frightened gargle. Fear replaced hatred.

"Now then," Wentworth nodded, "if you care to speak the words I want to hear, I'll permit you to talk again. Otherwise, I'm afraid I shall have to silence you permanently. It would really be a kindness to the good old English language."

19

Ram Singh came soundlessly to Wentworth's elbow and crouched with his eyes fixed on the prisoner.

"The Hindus," Wentworth said conversationally, "have some unique methods of torture. The victim usually dies, but not too quickly. Now tell me the name of your chief and his address."

"The mayor," gasped the prisoner, "The mayor!" He gave a Park Avenue address.

Wentworth shook his head, frowning. Whatever the Mayor of New York might do, he would not form an alliance with the Underworld.

"That's not the mayor's address," he said flatly. The sword point pricked flesh.

"For gawd's sake," whimpered the man. "I didn't mean it was de Mayor of New York. De boss calls hisself de Mayor and I give youse straight goods. Dar's his address."

Wentworth knew truth when he heard it. "Keep him prisoner, Ram Singh," he said quietly. "The police may want to question him a bit."

Ram Singh spoke in Punjabi, "They were coming up the dumbwaiter shaft, *sahib*, even as you predicted. They will not come up there any more."

A hard light leaped into Wentworth's eyes. He nodded slowly. He moved in a crouch toward the house. Ram Singh's whisper followed him.

"Master, do you wish to ask this rat more questions?"

There was menace in the Hindu's voice and Wentworth whirled about. The prisoner's voice rose in a shrill wail of fear and it ended in a liquid gurgle. Ram Singh glided away toward the house also, slipping his knife back into its sheath.

"He tried to kill you with a gun, Master," the Sikh said humbly, "and he was a rat."

WENTWORTH MOVED on toward the ruins of the house. The Spider never showed mercy in his dealings with criminals, why should the Spider's man?… Jackson stood as before in the hallway. He turned a smiling, wide-jawed face.

"Another squad came up, sir. I dropped them too."

Wentworth nodded. "Ram Singh, gas masks. Bring the police in, strip off their uniforms."

Jackson's smile broadened. "Retreat, sir?"

Wentworth's answering smile was faint, and bitter. "Retreat, if you wish to call it that. I shall be a fugitive."

The words ate into Wentworth's soul. No need to guess what construction would be put upon his flight. Wentworth laughed shortly. Once he was out of this death trap, he would have business with the "mayor!"

He drew on the gas mask Ram Singh presently brought him, signed to Jackson and Ram Singh to don police uniforms. Jenkyns was to remain behind, for once Wentworth left the building—he had small hope of escaping undetected—the attack would end.

Five minutes later, Wentworth entered the elevator, apparently the prisoner of two policemen. Ram Singh held a handkerchief to his face to hide his beard. They would gasp out something about gas to explain that.

There were handcuffs clasped loosely about Wentworth's

"Tell me the name of your
master, and his address!"

wrists. He could slip them off in no time at all and his automatics were tucked into his waist-band where he could reach them readily. It was queer that he thought of guns against the police, he who always before would have chosen death to using lethal weapons against them. A strange doubt, an overwhelming suspicion had entered his mind. Were the forces of the law allied with the Underworld? He was far from certain that the police would not kill him on sight....

The first floor corridor of the apartment building was jammed with police. A deep mutter of satisfaction went up as Jackson and Ram Singh thrust him out of the elevator and shoved toward the main door. A lane opened for their passage. Then a man's voice rose shrilly, almost hysterical with discovery. The policeman pointed at Jackson with a trembling hand.

"That man! He's got Pat's badge, but it isn't Pat!"

His words silenced the murmur, froze men in their tracks.

"Forward!" the Spider cried. He whipped his wrists free of the cuffs, caught out his automatics and blasted two shots toward the ceiling. In a flying wedge, he and Jackson and Ram Singh charged for the doors. For an instant, the ranks of police parted. Then they closed in again. Blackjacks were raised, nightsticks swished in.

A policeman braced himself in Wentworth's path, wide shoulders hunched forward, revolver against his hip. Jackson took the cop in a head-long dive. The gun blasted and a man moaned. Ram Singh's knife glinted high, but he used only the hilt. For a moment, a space was cleared.

Wentworth glanced about. They were twenty feet from the

main doors, a scant ten from the elevator. The police were packing ever thicker ahead of him.

"Back!" he whispered to the two who fought beside him. "We'll never make it forward."

HE WHIRLED and with his automatics lacing out felled three police. In two long strides he reached the door of the elevator. Jackson and Ram Singh crowded on his heels. Revolvers crashed deafeningly in the confined space as the door slammed shut. Wentworth threw the lever, sent the cage upward, stopped it abruptly at the third floor and sprang out. He glanced over his shoulder. His men were following, but Jackson's face was white and beaded with perspiration. His left hand was pressed hard into his side.

"Go on, sir," Jackson gasped. "Go on. I'll hold them off. I'm gone anyway."

Wentworth sprang to Jackson's side, and with a quick heave had the man across his shoulders. Obeying a jerk of Wentworth's head, Ram Singh hurled himself against a door. It crashed open at the second blow and they went through. Ram Singh stayed behind a moment to wedge the door shut, then overtook Wentworth at a window.

"Start a fire on the floor," Wentworth said calmly.

Ram Singh sprang to the draperies of the apartment they had entered, dumped cushions from a davenport atop them and struck a match. He ripped pages from a book and fed the flames. They licked up eagerly. Black smoke billowed against the ceiling. Wentworth eased Jackson to his feet.

"Ram Singh," Wentworth said, "make a sling and lower Jackson out of the window. The police outside won't know about your fake uniforms yet. They'll help and you two can easily escape."

Jackson was leaning weakly against the wall, hand and tunic stained with blood.

"Won't do it," he gasped.

Wentworth whirled toward him. "You'll do it," he snapped, "or I'll knock you cold and send you out anyway. Ram Singh!"

Ram Singh went down on one knee. "Please, master," he said swiftly. "We can all escape. We will not go without you."

Wentworth's face was strained, grayish beneath his tan. "Fool," he said acidly, "You'll ruin us all. Get out of the window and I will escape. I cannot burden myself with fools."

Ram Singh's eyes were stricken. "Master!" he cried. He looked into Wentworth's burning gaze, drew to his feet and touched his forehead with cupped hands. "I hear and obey," he whispered.

Jackson lashed him with curses as Ram Singh snatched a drape and tried to tie it beneath his arms, struck out furiously with his revolver. Wentworth reached him in a stride.

"It is our only chance, Jackson—my only chance," he said swiftly.

Jackson was past reason, with the pain of his wound, with the thought of deserting the man he had served through so many years. He lifted the revolver.

"You'll go with me, sir," he said, panting, "or I'll shoot you and carry you."

It was madness, though loyal madness. Wentworth's fist flashed, piled Jackson unconscious upon the floor. He knelt beside him, tied the drapery like a rope. His mouth was set in a straight thin line. His eyes were narrowed. There was a stinging in his eyeballs.

"Smoke's damned thick," he muttered. "Damned thick."

He got to his feet, met the pleading eyes of Ram Singh.

"Damn it to hell," Wentworth raged at him. "Get out of here. Get out quickly!"

RAM SINGH stooped over Jackson and lifted the powerful body easily to the window, lowered him on the drape. Police-men ran forward below, caught Jackson and eased him tenderly to the ground.

"You'll have to fight him clear, Ram Singh," Wentworth said shortly.

Ram Singh dropped to his knee, caught up Wentworth's hand and pressed it to his bearded lips. "If they kill you, Master," he whispered, his harsh voice rising, "I shall kill fifty men to pay for it, fifty, nay, a thousand, of their foolish throats shall…."

"Go, Ram Singh."

Ram Singh staggered to the window from which smoke was puffing, black and choking. He tied a drape to a chair leg, braced the chair across the opening as he climbed out and slid down with his face to the wall. He had a handkerchief between his teeth, and when he landed, he pressed it to his lips, coughing, coughing.

Well back from the window, Wentworth watched them go,

watched Ram Singh stagger along beside Jackson as they carried him to an ambulance, saw both men shoved inside. He nodded to himself. Ram Singh played his cards well. He would wait until the ambulance was well away, then overpower the few men in it....

Wentworth turned away from the window and, unashamed, brushed a tear from his cheek. Loyal men!

The door of the apartment crashed in. Wentworth dropped to his knees, peering through the smoke. It eddied about him thickly, then rushed in a solid cloud toward the door on the breast of the draft. The heat was intolerable, tears from the smoke streamed down Wentworth's face. He lifted his head and choked out a hoarse scream.

"Help!" he screamed. "In God's name, help, I'm fall—"

Then he crept away toward the dining room, across that into the kitchen. The smoke was thinner here and he scrambled into the dumbwaiter shaft, braced himself while he groped for the ropes. They were gone and he remembered then what Ram Singh had said:

"They were coming up the dumbwaiter. They will not come again."

Ram Singh had cut the rope. Wentworth laughed bitterly. So his best-laid plans were to fail! He choked down the laughter, coughed stranglingly. He was despairing too soon. He ducked back into the kitchen, found a servant's room and rapidly knotted sheets together. Laboriously then, he let himself down the dumbwaiter shaft, until his feet came to rest upon something—something that was soft and yielding.

He bent over in the circumscribed area and felt about him. A man lay crushed and dead atop the dumbwaiter, where he had fallen when Ram Singh cut the cables that operated the miniature elevator. Wentworth smiled thinly, looped the sheet beneath the arms of the man, then went back up his improvised rope hand over hand over hand. It was strenuous work, even for his superb strength to haul that body to the third floor, and when he achieved it, the room was choking with smoke, little tongues of red flame were pushing in beneath the door.

WENTWORTH BOUND a handkerchief over his mouth as he worked, changing clothing and jewelry with the dead man. He even placed his automatics with their registered numbers, upon the corpse and took for his own a forty-five caliber belly-gun with a sawed-off barrel which the man carried. Bones were broken in the corpse, but Wentworth counted on collapse of the flooring to cover that discrepancy. He looked about him, nodded slowly to himself, then lifted the body and bore it before him toward the swing door that opened into the adjoining room.

Flame and heat leaped at him when he opened the door, licked at his hands so that he had to bite his lips to choke back a cry of pain. He heaved the body straight into the midst of a gout of flame. For an instant, the fire was fanned out, then it sprang back, brighter, more furious than ever. Wentworth darted back to the kitchen, beat out the flames that licked from his clothing in a half-dozen places. He paused a moment by the gas stove, turning all the jets wide open, then he went again to the dumb-waiter shaft and clambered downward.

It was deadly work, getting back the dumbwaiter box. He had

to descend, get hold of the rope upon its top, then climb back to the first floor and haul it past the doorway there. Going down again, he supported the box upon his head until he could step out into the basement. The dumbwaiter shaft was thick with smoke. He groped his way across the basement, hesitated inside the outer door. Thick blackness there. Police patrols would be on the street, probably someone was lurking here, too.

Wentworth pulled the cap he had taken from the dead man down over his eyes, slipped along the wall. He held the belly-gun in his right hand and his keen eyes stabbed about him in the darkness. He made the end of the air-court, peered along the narrow alley that led to the street. That way was too dangerous, but directly opposite him was a window that opened into the basement of the adjoining apartment house. He dodged across the passageway and crouched before it, feeling the frame to determine how it opened....

Bullets smashed down on the pavement beside Wentworth. He could tell by the chattering speed of the shots that it was a Thompson sub-machine gun somewhere four or five stories above the street. He worked desperately. Even in the darkness, it was incredible that he should continue to escape the fusillade. The pounding of lead crept away to his right, swung back. Good God, he had to reach cover, at once! Wentworth spun about, kicked out the window, and.... The bullet hammered him flat down on the pavement. Striking his left shoulder, it raked tearingly down his ribs. His entire side went instantly numb.

Wentworth's lips shrank back from his teeth. He was flat on the pavement, his face against the cold concrete, his left arm twisted agonizingly beneath him. There was no pain yet, but he knew what was to come. Blood was warm across his chest. There was a heavy lethargy in his brain. He strained his right arm upward and fired the belly-gun. Fool! He cursed himself on the instant. Another bullet struck his ribs low down on the right hand side in back. He felt that he was nailed to the ground, pinned down by leaden spikes. His breath whistled between locked teeth….

WHY, GOOD God, he was being killed! That hose of bullets squirting lead down here into the alley had found him twice in the body. At any moment, it might strike a vital spot. And he had betrayed himself with the useless belly-gun. There was no emotion within Wentworth at the recognition that death was very near, almost certain. Wounded as he was, he could scarcely force his laggard body up on hands and knees. He could feel a pool of blood warm against his belly. Was there no way out? Think, brain, think!

Yes, there was a way. That window behind him with the glass already kicked out, but could he make it, with this hostile lead eating his vitality? Useless to shoot upward at that gunman. The short barrel of the belly gun kept it from shooting straight. No, only one thing. The Spider must run for his life! Wentworth choked back crazy laughter, run, with those bullets in him. He wriggled feet first toward the window. Men were shouting in the street. He could hear the pound of heavy feet. Dear God! The pain had filled him now, sweeping in weakening hot waves over his entire body. His head swam.

He got his ankles, his shins, half through the window. Jagged glass was slicing into his flesh, but he scarcely felt it because of the other agony which was blazing in his body. Now his knees had slipped free of the wall, the glass was scratching his thighs.

"Oh God!" The cry was forced from Wentworth.

Another slug had hit him somewhere in the back. He did not know where but it made his whole body numb. Breath panted from his lungs in gasping sobs. The end. Dear God, it must not be the end. Not here in this dirty alley, lying on his face in the coal dust. The Spider was not destined for that. Wentworth willed his agonized body to worm backward through the window, but he was not sure that he moved at all. A burst of bullets broke to fragments on the concrete just inches from his skull and the tiny particles bit into his flesh, tore his lips and cheeks.

A wild, sobbing oath tore from Wentworth's lips. He thrust the belly gun upward and yanked the trigger until he no longer had any feeling in the hand. A bullet hit his arm, dead center, and the gun went out of his hand. Wentworth's flinch from that new wound did what his body had failed to do at his brain's orders. It edged him back through the window and he dropped into darkness.

He was scarcely conscious of falling on the floor, but he knew presently that he was on his feet fighting his way through darkness which was studded with crimson blossoms of flame. Behind him, somewhere, a muffled voice shouted:

"Kill him! Kill him! Shoot to kill!"

Creeping into the blackness with arms that flapped helplessly and the strength flowing out of him with his blood, the Spider threw back his head and laughed. The sound of his defiance was weak....

## CHAPTER 4
## THROUGH THE DARKNESS

T HE INTERVAL that followed—Wentworth did not know whether it was minutes or hours—was clouded in red agony. Somehow, he reeled away through the darkness while guns blazed behind him and men shouted words that soon became meaningless. Wentworth knew dully that soon he must reach some spot where he could receive medical care or he would bleed to death. He might die anyhow. His teeth gritted together against the pain that beat upon him in waves of white-hot fire. His senses fluttered, left him and returned reluctantly. But he would not surrender. He could not. It meant death.

There was just one hope left him. He must reach the criminals and claim sanctuary. If it were a large organization, they might think him some minor member wounded in the battle. If not—well, he was dying anyhow. The steps that led up from the cellar were each a yard high, and it was a terrific effort of will to raise his foot.

He reached a long hallway and shrank back into a cupboard beneath the steps. Policemen rushed past him in darkness. But he could not stay here. They would see the blood drops. He choked down laughter. Everywhere he went, he would leave that red trail of blood drops, like little Spider seals, behind him. He staggered out of the cupboard, went toward the front door.

If more police had come through then, he would have been a dead man, but the luck that had been so strongly against him seemed to turn at that moment. He went out of the door with no policeman nearer than a half block away.

He was seen, of course. Men came pelting toward him. A revolver whanged away, twice, three times. Wentworth ran with his arms swinging helplessly. There was a dull agony in the right one. That bullet must have broken the bone, he told himself. He reeled into a doorway and smoke burned into his lungs. A tongue of red fire danced up before his eyes. He was… back in his own apartment building!

The end. Yes, there could no longer be any doubt about it. He had thought his luck had turned but in his weakness he had run blindly back into the maw of destruction. He set his teeth upon his lip and walked toward the flames. If they were a narrow band, he might get past and be safe for a little while on the other side. If they were thick, he would die. But he was a dead man anyway.

He held his breath and walked into the flame. The raw fire seared his dangling hands, brushed across his face, his closed eyes. He tripped, recovered, and was through the band of blazing death. Beyond it, smoke was incredibly thick. Wentworth pressed his face against a wall and moved on, found a doorway and went through. It was an elevator. He shouldered the door shut, lunged his hip against the lever.

When the elevator stopped, he did not know, but he reeled out and stood swaying, looking blindly about. A man and a boy barged out of a doorway and stopped, shrinking back as if in fear. Then they saw how ravaged was the man before them.

Wentworth tried to lift his hands toward them and the agony stabbed at his heart. His legs went limp and he slipped down on the floor, his unwounded shoulder against the wall. He kept his eyes on the face of the man.

"For God's sake," he whispered, "save me from the police!"

The man came close, his eyes strangely gentle, and the darkness he had been fighting so long rushed on him in a swift, joyous charge, crashing against his skull like a sandbag. So this was death!

WENTWORTH HAD known torture, he had been wounded countless times before, but never had the agony been so enduring, never had his own strength seemed so feeble. There was one enduring thought in his mind, one memory. There was a woman whose violet eyes were upon him, whose cool hands were upon his forehead. He called her Nita.

God alone knew where Nita van Sloan was through these interminable spells of pain. He whispered her name in his sleep and in his agony. There came the time when he opened his eyes finally upon consciousness. He saw again the face of the man who had been there beside the elevator door and he thought he was still there. The man smiled, wry, pocked face lighting up.

"Damme," he said gruffly, "I kapt tellin' them you'd be pullin' through. Sure an' I appreciate your proving Patrick O'Rourke is no liar!"

Wentworth closed his eyes and slept then. In the days that followed, he learned in little snatches the things that had happened. He had not entered his own apartment house, but another which had caught fire from it. The man who called himself Patrick O'Rourke had been "paying a business call" as he put it, but Wentworth suspected it was nothing more nor less than sneak-thievery. He had taken Wentworth out the back way to a dilapidated old car in the back alley. He had charged the police lines….

"Sure, heaven lent a helping hand," said Pat O'Rourke, "or

we'd all died then."

A girl entered, a girl with smooth hair that glowed with fire and deep blue eyes. This would be the girl he had called Nita, this was… Wentworth laughed weakly.

"You," he said, "are the boy who was with O'Rourke there in the burning house."

When the girl smiled, her piquant beauty leaped at one, for it was a gamin smile that wrinkled her nose, strange on her quiet face.

"I learned some rare new curse words from you," she laughed, "but there were some I couldn't quite make out." She repeated awkward imitations of grand Hindu curses and Wentworth smiled at her again. He looked about him and found that the room in which he slept was all white and that there was a dressing table with a shirred pink skirt against the far wall and understood that he had been placed in the girl's own room.

The O'Rourkes, father and daughter, laughed at his stammering apologies. Pat leaned over and laid a strangely gentle hand on Wentworth's forearm.

"Sure, you're agin them devils of police who killed my son," he said, "and you got no passport from the Mayor of Hell, so…."

Wentworth's eyes narrowed at the strange term and his mind groped back into the hazy time before the curtain of pain had dropped upon him. The Mayor of Hell…. He remembered then the prisoner he had taken on the roof of his pent house gasping out that the leader of the overwhelming attack was called the Mayor….

"How long," Wentworth demanded, his voice sharpening, "how long have I been like this?"

PAT STRAIGHTENED, a fine broad figure of a man despite the graying of hair along the sides of his head. His face was very sober. "Six weeks."

Wentworth's good hand moved into a slow, stiff fist. "And what has happened in that time?"

"Lots of things," Pat informed him, "but we'll not be after discussing that now." He got up firmly and walked from the room. Wentworth watched the odd, solid way he walked, the pride with which he held his head, almost regal…. Well, in Ireland, the O'Rourkes had been kings.

Wentworth got the story slowly, until Pat realized that the

37

worry over not knowing was holding back Wentworth's recovery. Then he came in, sat solidly in a heavy oak chair and handed him a newspaper. " 'Tis the only one in town that held out against the Mayor of Hell," he said simply.

Wentworth pulled his eyes from Pat's grave face and studied the headlines.

HOEY PLANS NEW TEN MILLION STEAL!

The fat, block letters were spread across the entire width of the page and the details under it were sickeningly obvious—an appropriation for "special relief" which the paper declared was nothing more nor less than a payroll for the thugs in Hoey's employ. Hoey, he saw, was the new United States Senator who had been appointed to take the place of the previous official "killed in an automobile accident at the orders of the Mayor of Hell" the paper declared.

Wentworth's old friend, Stanley Kirkpatrick, had been impeached as Governor of the State on charges trumped up by Hoey. His present whereabouts were "unknown." There was a column which recited the day's crimes and a table showing the amount of crime since Hoey had been appointed senator and, said the story, "since the cold-blooded murder of the one man who might have averted all this, Richard Wentworth, who fought for humanity under the name of the Spider."

Wentworth's hands, the feeble right just emerging from its cast, began to tremble so that the paper rustled. So it was no longer a secret—his labors under the name of the Spider? The newspaper praised him as dead, but if he had been alive, that paper and all humanity would have been upon his heels to execute him for his hundred kills, even though each man he had slain had been some enemy of mankind.

Wentworth knew a brief spasm of agony. All this time, then, Nita van Sloan had mourned him as dead. Jackson and Ram Singh might have suspected he planned some escape, but his long continued silence would have convinced them he had failed. He realized suddenly, overwhelmingly, that with this new evil reign, they must continue to think him dead. The first breath of suspicion attaching to them and the Mayor of Hell would smash them instantly.

A RASPING curse forced itself out between Wentworth's teeth. "In God's name, Pat," he whispered, "how far has this thing gone?"

Pat had his thick, square-cut hands on his solid knees. "The whole distance," he said flatly. "Look at the date of that news-paper."

Wentworth looked, but it meant nothing to him. "I don't know what day this is," he said.

Pat laughed, but without mirth. "To be sure you don't," he said. "Well, that paper is two weeks old. The night after it was published, Hoey sent the National Guard to close the shop. It's been printed since, but it's Hoey's paper now. Sure, it's a miserable state we've come to."

Wentworth sank back upon his pillows and closed his eyes. "Pat, can you get me newspapers back to the night you found me? There should be some money in my pockets, and if there isn't…." He checked his words, realizing with overwhelming

PAT
O'ROURKE

KATHLEEN

LEN ROBERTS

SENATOR HOEY

suddenness that there was no more for him. Richard Wentworth was dead. He laughed sharply. "If there isn't, Pat, we'll get some as soon as I can navigate."

Pat looked shamefaced. "There's some, sorr, though not much. We're poor folks and I've used a bit to take care of you. Not a penny for ourselves, by the Holy Mother."

"I'm sure you haven't," Wentworth said heartily. Pat smiled with the lighting of his whole face that was like his daughter's. "Sure, it's good to be mistook for an honest man," he boomed.

For a full minute, Wentworth studied the face of the Irishman. He knew that O'Rourke was a small-time crook of some kind and it seemed that the girl must be in it with him. Yet, he was a kindly man who had saved the life of a stranger and it was hard to think evil of the girl.... Wentworth's work was clear. Even if he had not been the Spider, if his life had not been pledged to the defense of his people, he would have risen against the Mayor of Hell. Yet, eager as he was for the battle, he could not fight alone. The strength was not in him.

"Patrick O'Rourke," Wentworth said. "Will you help me to destroy this Mayor of Hell?"

Pat's face was paled fleetingly by fear. He glanced over his shoulder. "For Sweet Mary's sake, sorr," he bent closer whispering. "Don't speak so loud! But tell me.... What do you mean?"

Wentworth put a hand on his arm. "Pat, this Mayor of Hell has ruined and almost killed me. So long as he is in power, neither you, nor your daughter, nor anyone else is safe."

Pat nodded, "True for you, sorr."

"Well then, Pat?"

O'Rourke got up and went to the door. "Kathleen," he called, his deep voice rumbling. The girl came to the door presently, walked over to where Pat sat beside the bed with her nose crinkled in that cheerful gamin's smile. It faded quickly when she saw the set seriousness of their faces.

"Close the door, Kathleen," said Pat.

The girl's face paled a little. She shut the door and came back to the bed. Pat studied her eyes for along time.

"Daughter," he said heavily, "shall we fight the Mayor of Hell?"

Kathleen's deep blue eyes went to Wentworth's face. She walked swiftly from the room and when she came back she held the big hand of a man in police blue, a youngster like herself with a dark, serious face. His eyes went quickly to Wentworth, to Pat O'Rourke.

"What's up, sir?" he asked.

Kathleen drew the boy's arm about her waist, standing with her shoulders against his deep chest. "They want to know, Len, if we shall fight the Mayor of Hell?" She looked at Wentworth gravely. "Len is resigning from the police force. We just decided tonight. You see, we were going to be married soon, but Len can't stand the police force any longer. Since Hoey came to power, crooks have been enrolled on the force: even the honest men left have to let crooks go free. Today Len arrested a killer and they suspended him for it. Commissioner Fogarty is Hoey's man. The police killed young Pat and Len knows the men that did it. So… Well, what do you say, Len?"

Wentworth could see the policeman's arm tightening about Kathleen's waist, could see the determination hardening the lean, long line of his jaw. Len Roberts voice was very quiet, even light.

"Sure," he said, "it's a swell idea. Let's give the Mayor of Hell a taste of what hell is really like!"

## CHAPTER 5
## ARMY OF FORLORN HOPE

WENTWORTH FORCED himself to wait two weeks longer before beginning the attack—two weeks in which he studied the back copies of newspapers which Pat and Len Roberts got for him. He learned something about Nita there. She had come to the scene of the attack upon him when the fire was raging beyond control. There had been an attempt upon her life and she had killed the man with the automatic Wentworth had insisted she always carry. And she had almost had to stand trial for murder!

Fortunately, the power of the Mayor of Hell had not reached its full strength then. She had won free. Wentworth's fortune had been confiscated by the State, under a new law Hoey and his puppet, Governor Langson, had put through the terrified Legislature. Jackson and Ram Singh were in the penitentiary serving long terms for assisting a fugitive to escape…. Wentworth's hot rage became a cold fury within his brain. It would simmer there, he knew, until he had struck off the shackles of the Mayor of Hell from the people he loved.

It was a curious thing, but nowhere in any newspaper was any mention of the Mayor of Hell. Senator Hoey was everywhere, but that sinister figure behind the scenes was never called by name. Pat O'Rourke and Len Roberts could give no clue. No man they knew had even seen him, but his shadow lay like a blight upon everything.

It was the middle of December—two months and three weeks to the night since the evening when Wentworth had stood playing his violin in the face of death—that he called the first action meeting of his little army of forlorn hope. It was typical of the vitality, the commanding personality of the Spider, called Master of Men, that these men who did not even know his name should follow his lead without question.

Len Roberts stood behind Kathleen's chair, his hands upon her shoulders. Pat O'Rourke sat with his feet planted flat upon the floor, his thick hands on his knees and his gray-sprinkled head bowed forward thoughtfully. Wentworth walked restlessly up and down the room. He had been on his feet for three weeks now, had even ventured to walk upon the streets, for the sprinkling of bullet scrap which had powdered his face on that night of flame and disaster and death had given him a disguise his enemies were unlikely to penetrate—especially since they thought him dead.

Wentworth stopped his pacing, stood rigidly facing the two men. "We must become killers," he announced flatly. "There is no other scourge the men obeying the Mayor of Hell will fear. That does not mean we must kill defenseless men. It means that we pay the criminals back in their own coin. You must make up your minds to that.

"You, Len, you, Pat, are killing machines. If you do not kill, the other man will kill you. That is unavoidable. Kill first and—kill terribly!"

Wentworth turned to his bed, jerked aside the pillow and picked up three knives. They were long-bladed, edged like razors and upon the hilt of each a death's head had been carved. They were nine-inch Bowie knives of the ancient, murderous pattern. Kathleen's face whitened as she saw them, the eyes of Len Roberts and Pat O'Rourke grew hard.

"It's not a weapon to my liking," Pat said harshly, "but no more will it be to *theirs!* It is a good choice."

LEN ROBERTS, dressed in dark civilian clothes tonight,

took his without comment. Wentworth handed each a sheath.

"Inside your coat collar, between your shoulders," he explained. "Like this." He thrust the knife into his own sheath already attached in that position. He smiled at them suddenly, thinly. "The draw is like this."

His hand whipped over his shoulder. There was a flash of steel and the knife quivered in the floor between Pat O'Rourke's feet, its point embedded an inch deep. Len Roberts laughed shortly. He was looking down at his knife.

"We should have a mark," he said. "A seal they'd recognize, like the Spider's seal."

"A cross on their foreheads!" Pat O'Rourke boomed. "'Tis a holy war we fight. Put the emblem on their foreheads! They say the Holy Mark will exorcise devils, and sure we fight in hell."

Kathleen was on her feet, the color gone from her face so that her glowing hair seemed the more vivid by contrast.

"I want my knife, too," she interrupted.

Pat O'Rourke turned slowly toward his daughter, with pride on his face. Len Roberts said hoarsely, "No, not you, Kathleen."

Kathleen whirled toward him. "Do you think that if you fall, I want to live?" she demanded. "Do you think that if you are discovered, I shall have a chance to live? Surely, you know the Mayor of Hell and his devils better than that!"

Young Roberts' dark face was very pale. He shook his head dazedly, "Good God," he whispered. "What are we doing to you, Kathleen?"

She laughed at him. "Nothing," she averred. "You would be a poor coward if you delayed a minute on account of me. But I don't intend to be left behind." She whirled toward Wentworth. "That night there in the burning house. Pop hasn't told you, but I will. We were dirt-poor, starving, and young Pat tried to steal something. Pop followed and found him there. He's done the same thing himself. We can't starve, and unless you are one of the favored darlings of the politicians here you get nothing. And, damn them, *they killed Pat!* I want my knife." She paused after her long speech, her cheeks flushed, her blue eyes bright.

"It's not woman's work," Wentworth said. His voice was kind. He was thinking of another girl, the woman he loved, of the times when she had fought by his side.

Len Roberts put his hands on Kathleen's shoulders, but she shook them off. Pat O'Rourke said slowly, "It's like she says, Len. If we die, *they'll* see to it she don't keep on living long. Sure, she's an O'Rourke. Give her a knife."

Wentworth smiled and slipped a hand to his belt. He drew out a smaller knife. The handle was ivory, carved into a stalking tiger. He bowed with his strange, old-world courtesy as he handed it, hilt first, into her hand. She held it before her eyes, kissed the hilt. Her face was turned upward and in it blazed a glory and a curse. She said nothing at all.

"I expected this," Wentworth told her.

Pat said solemnly, "The O'Rourke women have fought beside their men before this." He turned to Wentworth. "We ought to have a name, like Len said, and we ought to know what we do first."

Wentworth nodded slowly, "We're not even a corporal's guard, but I'm Corporal Death from now on. We might call ourselves the Long Knives."

Pat O'Rourke nodded, "And this first job of ours?" His face was very grim and he fingered the knife.

Wentworth shook his head. "It isn't killing unless it's necessary. We've got to have money to operate. Tonight we get it."

"Where?"

Wentworth smiled. "Alderman Huntley is a very wealthy contractor. He's Hoey's spokesman in the city. I propose that we pay a visit to Alderman Huntley's wall safe… I knew Huntley."

Len Roberts looked troubled. "I don't like this. It's not… honest."

"Neither is Huntley," Wentworth told him shortly. "Don't worry about opening the safe. I'll do that. Kathleen, I hadn't figured you in on this. Do you mind very much if we leave you at home this time?"

Kathleen said, "I mind like everything, but I guess it can't be helped."

ALDERMAN JOHN HUNTLEY lived amid his constituency on the East Side. They lived in tenements under the Queensborough Bridge. He lived in Sutton Place, the abode of the wealthy. Just a block or so away, but miles apart in environment. His was a small, two-story house jammed between taller buildings. There was an alley in the back where his three-car garage, filled, was situated.

It was snowing, small hard granules driven by a stiff wind, when Wentworth went alone to the garage where the other two were to join him at intervals of ten minutes. There was a set, hard expression about Wentworth's mouth and his eyes held a cold gleam. Yes, he knew John Huntley, knew him well. Even in the days when Stanley Kirkpatrick had held the commissionership of police, Huntley had been crooked, the ally of the Underworld. It hadn't been possible to get evidence against him.

The chauffeurs—there were two of them—had rooms above the garage. They were both gunmen of unsavory reputation. One of them had done time for manslaughter. Like master, like men. The Spider—but he was Corporal Death now—would feel small compunction about making them the first victims of the Long Knives, should they interfere with his plans. But he would have to be careful. He had only a small, cheap revolver, and the knife. He would have to use the knife left-handed, since his right arm was still stiff and weak from being wounded, despite continuous exercise.

The garage would be protected with burglar alarms, of course, but Wentworth doubted that they were as good—or as widespread—as those on the house. It was unlikely, for instance, that the bedrooms of the two men would be wired… Wentworth's wounds gave him a twinge as he swung up the drainpipe at one corner of the garage. His right arm he could use only sparingly and the fingers of his left were strained by the weight upon them.

But presently, he had his feet upon a pipe brace and his head on a level with a window. It was shut and, peering in, Wentworth could make out the vague loom of furniture. It was a sitting-room.

Wentworth got a hand upon its sill and presently was standing there precariously. He reached to the roof gutter. This was the most perilous part of the climb, for he would be forced to

depend now on his weakened right arm for help. He got both hands on the cold gutter, and his breath pushed out in a gasp as the pain shot through his flesh. But he persisted. He muscled his body upward, got his left elbow in the gutter. After that, it was comparatively easy. The roof slanted very little and snow had not stuck there. He lay flat, panting silently. The snow bit against his cheeks as he stared toward the darkness of the main house. SILENTLY, HE wriggled across the roof, peered over at the windows at the back of the garage. One was opened about half-way. Wentworth nodded. It was as he had thought. He twisted about, hung down beside the window and got a toe upon the sill. He let go with his right hand to seize the window frame and—a voice spoke from within!

"Just stay like dat, buddy, until I glim your pan!" Wentworth did not need to see the man to know that he held a gun in his fist—or to understand that it was one of Huntley's gunman chauffeurs.

"Geez," Wentworth whined, in imitation of the other's accent, "youse sounds like a pal. Let me…" He caught the window frame, drew himself close against the glass, stood there, exaggerating his panting distress. He could see the man now, a vague shadow inside the window.

"I ain't no pal of yourn," the man snarled. "Put up your hands."

Wentworth groaned, "Geez, I'll fall, pal…."

"No kidding?" the man inside chuckled. Then his voice turned ugly. "Put 'em up, or I'll blow your guts out through your back. Come on, up wit "em."

Wentworth whined and pleaded, lifted his left hand reluctantly from his grip upon the window frame. There was no hope now that the alarm would not be given. Already, he was sure, the second chauffeur must be awake. Well, he must chance it, pin everything on one desperate hope….

"Hurry up," growled the man inside. "It will maybe only break an arm or somethin' if you fall, and a bullet in your belly will kill you. Dis here is a forty-five."

Wentworth whimpered, "Okay, pal, okay. Just give me a chanct…."

He whipped a hand over his shoulder and the knife came out glittering. It crashed through the glass, and Wentworth swung sharply to the left, clear of the window. A bullet could still reach him, but he was at least not directly in front of the gun muzzle. He had no way of telling whether or not the knife had struck right after crashing the glass. True, he had put all his strength into the quick downward whip of his hand....

Glass crashed and tinkled to the floor and to the ground. Inside, a man groaned in awful pain. A thick, strangled curse.... Wentworth whipped back to the sill, jerked up the window and jumped lightly to the floor inside. The chauffeur was plucking at the handle of the knife, half-buried in the base of his throat. He saw Wentworth and his face contorted horribly. He strained his gun upward.... Wentworth stepped alertly forward, took the gun from weakened fingers. The man pitched forward on his face, writhed and was still.

The heavy automatic he had retrieved was a comfort in Wentworth's hand. He stole toward the door that led into a bathroom and through that into the other chauffeur's room. He could not understand the silence unless, unless.... The other chauffeur was out! Wentworth hurried back to the room where the dead man lay. There was a light, hazed by falling snow, in the main house. A window screeched up.

"Anything wrong out there?" a man's voice called. "Shall I call the police?"

Wentworth thickened his accent, and miraculously, it was as if the dead man spoke. "Aw, close your trap," he said roughly. "We was just having a little clean fun."

THE WINDOW slammed down in obvious exasperation and Wentworth smiled to himself there in the darkness. If his

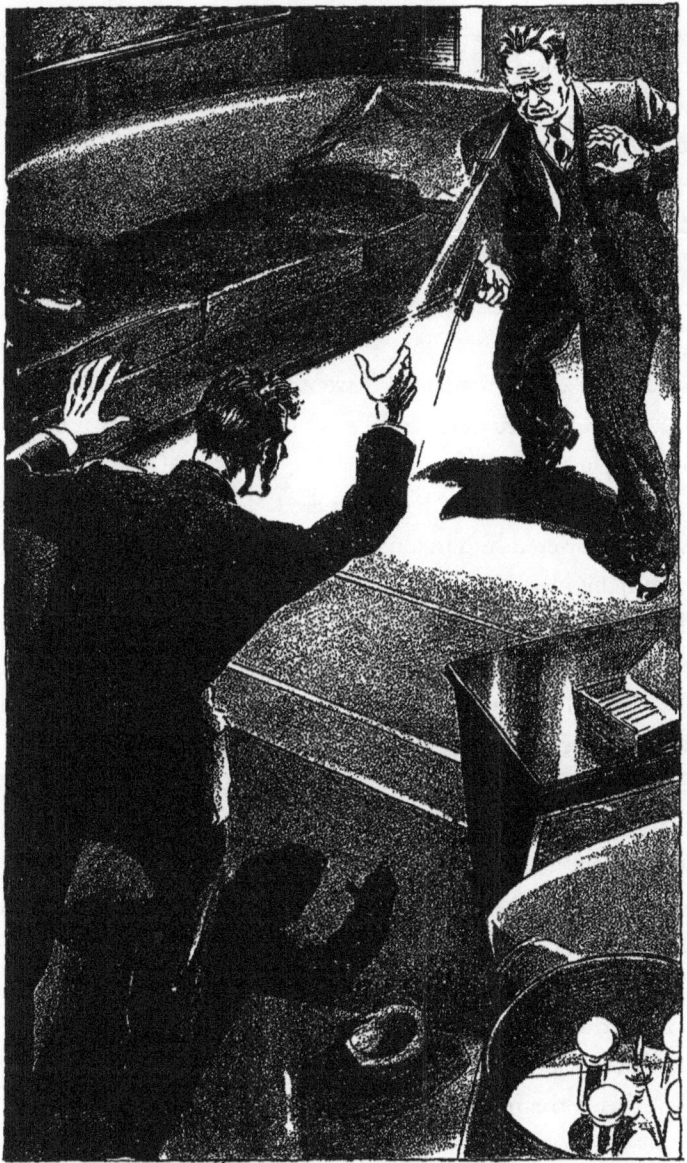

Alderman Huntley screamed as Corporal Death's knife flashed through the air!

body was enfeebled from the long confinement of his wounds, at least his brain worked as keenly as ever. He bent and pulled the dead man over on his back, wrenched the knife from the wound. His lips grinned back from his teeth, then. The chauffeur's face was not a pretty sight. He thought that the city would know a horror of Corporal Death when the morning came....

Wentworth hurriedly found keys in the dead man's pockets and went downstairs. There were two automobiles there, a heavy sedan and a sport roadster. He went to the outer door. When he opened it, Len Roberts and Pat O'Rourke entered as if blown by the blustering wind.

"Heard glass break," Pat whispered. "I was afraid...?" Wentworth answered him in almost normal tones. "I had to kill the chauffeur. He's a jail bird, a killer. He has the cross of Corporal Death upon his face." He gave them no chance to comment, but raced on. "There will be another chauffeur here with Alderman Huntley after a while. Let Huntley come to the house. Hold the chauffeur here. You'd better wear masks over your faces. Understand?"

O'Rourke nodded slowly, his eyes on Wentworth's face in the dim light of the flashlight Wentworth held. "Is this other chauffeur a bad one, too?" he asked quietly. His breath made a frosty cone from his lips.

Wentworth turned to Roberts. "You remember the killing of Heine Burkan?" he asked quietly.

Roberts jerked out a "Yes!" between locked teeth.

"This is the man who served two years for it," Wentworth

said. "You know his record, know that he has got off for a dozen murders."

Roberts' face was immensely relieved. "Oh, that's the kind of eggs they are!" he said. "I didn't like killing him much before…."

Wentworth told him grimly, "You'll like it even less after you see him. If you want to cut out, Roberts, this is the time to say so."

Roberts shook his head. "No, I'm with you. Don't pay any attention if I'm a little squeamish. I—I've never killed a man."

Wentworth clapped him on the shoulder, moved off toward the door that opened on the inner yard. "Keep out of sight," he called back softly, "Cover your faces. Remember our places."

There hadn't been any house key on the ring in the chauffeur's pocket, so Wentworth knocked on the door and presently the window opened again.

"What do you want?"

The snow was falling more thickly and it hid the man at the window, concealed Wentworth.

"Come down and open the door, mug," Wentworth snarled, still in the voice of the dead chauffeur.

The man argued, but when Wentworth threatened to smash in the door, the butler evidently assumed he was drunk and came down. With a gun in his belly, the butler surrendered without a sound. He was bound and gagged, stuffed into a closet, then Wentworth proceeded to the judge's study where the wall safe was situated. It took him a half hour to open it, for he was without the usual tools of the Spider. He was in luck and stuffed some twenty thousand dollars in currency into his pockets, locked the safe again, wiped it clean of fingerprints.

Then Wentworth selected one of the Alderman's long panatelas and lighted it, mixed a scotch-and-soda from the cellaret, settled into a chair to wait.

It was an hour before Alderman Huntley entered by the front door. Wentworth heard him dusting snow from his coat, stamping and blowing in the hall. Then, as Wentworth had expected, he saw the dim light from his study and came directly there. He started back, his heavy, florid face darkening, then whipped out a short, ugly revolver.

"What in the hell are you doing here?" Alderman Huntley demanded.

Wentworth did not rise. He smiled, laid his second cigar upon the table beside him.

"Waiting for you," he said gently.

Alderman Huntley came forward on slow, careful feet. There was bewilderment as well as anger in his small, wary eyes.

"You've got a hell of a nerve," he said sharply. "I suppose you came from… *him?*"

Wentworth shook his head, got slowly to his feet. "Not at all, Huntley," he said. "I am Corporal Death, and I have come to kill you!"

## CHAPTER 6
## THE BEST LAID PLANS

A LDERMAN JOHN HUNTLEY looked at Wentworth incredulously with his small, hard eyes and something like a smile touched his fat lips. He was dapper, precise in bearing, despite double chins, and his pince-nez glasses glinted almost mockingly. He looked over this man with the empty hands very slowly.

"Well, well," he said pleasantly, "it is nice of you to give me warning in advance."

He started forward, still moving cautiously, with the revolver held low against his hip. It was his obvious intention to reach the telephone and call help.

"Before I kill you," Wentworth said quietly, "I shall want your passport."

Huntley started to laugh, but something in the deadly serious mien of the man before him stayed his mirth. He stopped and gripped his gun more tightly.

"I think it will be better if you raise your hands," he said, "and on second thought, I don't think I shall call the police. I don't like the way you talk. A bullet...."

The man who called himself Corporal Death smiled cheerfully. "Exactly! You wish me to raise my hands first?" He lifted them shoulder-high, close to his head. He could draw his knife in a flash this way. Huntley stood squarely before him, his little eyes opening and narrowing strangely.

57

"Now, Corporal Death," he said, "just why are you asking questions?"

Corporal Death nodded, his tones surprised. "For information, of course. Who is the Mayor of Hell, Alderman?"

Huntley took a half-step forward. "I thought so—a government spy!" he breathed. Then his face twisted. "Take it, fool, you thought—"

Alderman Huntley screamed and reeled backward as Corporal Death's knife flashed through the air and made two lightning slashes. The gun blasted thunderously and the glass door of a bookcase collapsed behind Wentworth. But Huntley did not shoot again. He was crouched forward with his hands clasped to his face. *He screamed, screamed!* Little threads of blood made a tracery over his fingers.

Wentworth stepped back to the light and switched it off. When the two policemen who had been on guard in front of the house crashed in the front door, setting a dozen alarm bells jangling, Wentworth was flat against the floor beside the desk. A flashlight beam cut through the air and picked out the agonized figure of Huntley.

"What's the matter, Alderman?" one of the police cried.

They surged forward, holding the light on Huntley. One of them caught his wrist and pulled a hand away from the bleeding face. The policeman cried out hoarsely then and reeled backward....

"Corporal Death is here!" Wentworth made his voice hollow and booming, muffled his mouth with his hand so that the sound might seem to come from anywhere.

The two policemen whirled in a dazed circle. One of them fired crazily, at nothing. Wentworth laughed, with a flat mocking intonation. He stood just behind Alderman Huntley. He leaned forward and whispered: *"The Cross of Corporal Death!* How do you like it, Alderman?"

**HUNTLEY SCREAMED** and lunged forward. The two police pivoted toward him, shooting, and the alderman went down without a cry. Wentworth had dodged aside. He had his gun in his hand and, deliberately, he shot a leg out from under each policeman.

He thought happily that his aim was as perfect as ever. "A warning from Corporal Death," he breathed. "Be honest, take no more bribes, or you, too, will bear—*the Cross of Corporal Death!"*

Wentworth left the two men screaming when he slid through the door of the study and sped light-footed through the house. Women's voices were crying out somewhere there above and thinly, through thick walls, came the hysteria of a police whistle. It took only seconds to reach the garage. Roberts was in the uniform of the captured chauffeur and he whipped open the doors, sprang to the wheel. Wentworth and Pat O'Rourke climbed into the back and half-drew the curtains. The big limousine rolled quietly down the alley, turned toward Sutton Place.

A policeman sprang into the street. Roberts leaned out and spoke gravely. "Alderman Huntley's car," he said. "The Alderman's got an important date *downtown.* He shot a burglar a moment ago in the garage."

The policeman stepped back stammering and Wentworth for all the smooth success of his escape plan, felt a sharp, burning rage mount within him. Damn it, the whole police force must be under the thumb of the Mayor of Hell.

"That… cross," Pat O'Rourke whispered. "Good God! We saw the chauffeur."

Wentworth's lips twisted. "Terror is something they can understand, Pat. They will learn to fear the Cross of Corporal Death."

"Holy Mother!" said Pat O'Rourke. He moved his hand swiftly in the sign of the cross, then shuddered. "You've changed the meaning of it… Corporal Death."

Wentworth nodded briskly. "I'll be back later." He leaned forward and tapped the glass behind Roberts. The car stopped and he climbed out. "Ditch this car soon, Roberts. It won't take them long to spread the alarm."

Roberts' face was white. "Yes, Corporal Death."

The car rolled away and Wentworth watched its tail-light blur in the thickening snow before he walked back along the street. He found the window he had spotted and entered a late pawn-shop to dicker for the time-blackened violin he had spotted as he passed. His hands ached for the touch of it, and his soul longed for the release that music gave him. He had done assassin's work tonight and the reek of it, the screams, were a thing that a man wanted to get out of his ears. He remembered that women had cried out up above there in Huntley's home. That was the hell of a man's misdeeds. They always kicked back that way upon the innocent.…

WENTWORTH BARGAINED swiftly for the violin, then, with the case in his hand, he took a taxi to the brightest corner of Broadway. The cab moved silently over streets which were coating with snow. On Broadway, men in crimson Santa Claus suits were ringing bells by iron pots. There was a tall Christmas tree at Times Square. The realization that within another ten days it would be Christmas struck Wentworth with a feeling of amazement and pain. The happiest season of the year, and the town writhed in the grip of a base, murderous criminal dictator.

The man on the streets wasn't suffering terribly yet, except in the terrific mounting of taxes, but wait a while until robbers left their victims dead in the streets and the police turned deaf ears to complainants, or told the crooks where to find the witnesses they must murder to stay free. They would understand then. "Merry Christmas! Happy New Year!"

Wentworth rapped on the glass and got out on Times Square, the pavement where the slim triangle of the Times Building raised its head. He shuffled, in his character of an itinerant violin player, around to the sheltered side of the building, where the snow danced aimlessly in the wind-eddies and there he took his stand. It was cold weather for a violinist, but nimble fingers kept themselves warm. He began to play....

It was relief in his soul which sang from the instrument and many were those who turned to stare at this scar-faced man with the hunched shoulders who played so hauntingly. Wentworth's teachers had wrung their hands over his refusal to make a profession of music. He might have been the world's greatest virtuoso, they told him, but other work had called—the purging of the Underworld.... Wentworth had a plan in coming here to play. He knew that in such monstrous organizations as the Mayor of Hell's contrived to extend their graft even to the street corner peddlers and he thought that, perhaps, he could form contact here with some minion of the Mayor.

His eyes glanced about him brightly, scanning the passing crowd. Wentworth was a genius of disguise, not because he was skillful with pigments and artificial hair, though he excelled in that, too, but because he could completely assume the character of the person he sought to impersonate. Now, he was entirely the street violin-player, half-servile, half-contemptuous of the crowd from whom his cap, lying upside down on the snow, cadged coins. He exaggerated the movements of his bow, swayed the violin in the manner of vaudeville players. He got attention; he got coins. Ultimately, he was sure, he would meet a hireling of the Mayor....

Wentworth did not believe in Destiny as a regulator of men's lives any more than he trusted to luck to win his battles for him. But Destiny took a hand in his affairs tonight. A woman, passing in a taxi-cab, leaned forward and signaled her driver to stop. She alighted from the automobile and strolled casually toward where Wentworth stood playing. Wentworth saw her, as he saw everyone who passed him there on the pavement and his heart leaped into his throat and throbbed there achingly. There was no mistaking the easy grace of the woman's carriage, nor the proud lift of her head, nor, as she came closer, the quiet distinction of her dress beneath the sable coat, the matchless deep violet of her eyes. It was the one woman on earth who knew his secrets, and whom he loved, Nita van Sloan.

And she had recognized him! There could be no doubt about that. He had never been able to disguise himself from her loving eyes, and there had been no attempt to disguise the brilliant technique of the violin playing which she loved. Yes, she recognized him, and she was strolling toward him now, pretending not to look at him at all, but studying the sign-boards of the motion picture show across the street, the news sign above his head. A trembling seized Wentworth. Oh, to have a few minutes with Nita, to touch the sweet warmth of her lips….

HE COULD imagine the shocked incredulity with which Nita had heard his music. She would not have believed he was dead, never, despite his jewelry and guns found in the ruins. He had been missing, believed dead, before this in his battles with the Underworld. His long silence would have tried her faith, but in her secret, inner heart, she would never have quite believed, and then—to hear the music of her lover sing to her out of the gabble of Times Square!

Looking at her as she moved toward him, he who knew every turn of her hand could see the tension of her body, could recognize how she suffered, walking toward him. She still was not sure! Wentworth knew that she could never reveal her recognition unless he gave the sign and he knew that he must not do it now. Even as he stared hungrily at the woman he loved, he was aware that an automobile had slowed to the curb across the street and that a man had alighted, was staring toward him. Not that it necessarily meant anything, but the Spider had learned caution in a hard school.

Well, it would not hurt to let Nita be sure. She would not

betray her discovery any more than she had already. Wentworth ceased the intricate thing he was playing with a flourish and swung into a tender love song that she had always loved, that he had often played to her. He drew the dulcet notes from the violin with fingers of love and Nita, now at last, was sure. He saw her grope in her purse as she stood before him, as if fumbling for a coin. But her eyes were raised to his, burning, burning. She could not help see how wasted, how sick he had been. Nita's white teeth set upon her lip. Her bronze-glinting curls trembled with her effort to remain silent.

Dick gazed straight into her eyes and played and played. Oh, for just a word, just a minute with her! Nita dropped a quarter into his cap. Her head was down and she stumbled once as she went blindly away. Wentworth tore his eyes away from her departing back and found that the man who had alighted from an automobile across the street was standing squarely before him, hands thrust deep into his overcoat pockets, eyes hard and unblinking beneath his derby brim.

He said nothing at all and Wentworth took the violin down, as if timidly, from beneath his chin. There was a throbbing pain in his right temple where there was an old knife scar. It was a signal of danger. This was no graft collection man of the Mayor of Hell. He knew that without quibbling. This was a man who had been following Nita, undoubtedly to see if she still had contact with the men of the Spider. The Underworld had never been able to believe that he worked alone. And now Nita's love had set this trap....

The man in the derby stooped and picked up the quarter Nita had thrown into the cap, inspected both sides with hard eyes.

"That's my quarter, mister," Wentworth used a beggar's whine. "You wouldn't take money from a poor man, would you, mister? Wouldn't you like me to play you something?"

"Button your lip," the man said flatly. "Pack up that fiddle and come along."

"I've got to stay here and play, Mister, I got to earn my living...."

The man stepped close and put his button eyes on Wentworth's. "You come along, or there'll be trouble, see?"

Wentworth bent over his violin case and made his hands tremble. He tried to tell himself that this was a piece of luck, but inside of him, his heart was cold. This would undoubtedly put him in the hands of some of the Mayor's men, but if they even suspected that he was connected with the Spider.... A heavy car rolled to the curbing and Wentworth was thrust into it. There were two men there with guns in their hands and—*there was Nita!*

Wentworth was thrust roughly into the seat beside her. He edged away, muttering, "Excuse me, lady."

The man who had brought him to the car laughed. "That ain't no lady," he said, "that's the Spider's widow. The Black Widow. I don't suppose you know that, do you?"

Wentworth tried to stall, but fear was a cold, writhing knot within him. His disguise was the thinnest. Where he was being taken, there undoubtedly would be one crook who would know the face of Richard Wentworth, the Spider!

NITA VAN SLOAN

# CHAPTER 7
## THE MAYOR'S QUESTION

**H**UDDLED OVER his violin case, Wentworth sent
sly glances about. Under the guise of timorousness, he
sought to calculate the chances of escape. Three men, two of
them with guns in their hands. Even alone, he would hesitate

to attack them, but with the almost certainty that if it came to shooting, Nita would be hit, it was out of the question. Besides there was a chance that he might be brought face to face with the Mayor....

"Did you frisk the mug?" demanded a man in the front seat.

The gunman in the derby grunted a negative. "Naw, Damn fool even to take this mug in."

"I'm running this, Slick," the first man said quietly. "Frisk him."

Wentworth's lips tightened, his muscles set rigidly. He was remembering suddenly that he had the twenty thousand dollars taken from Alderman Huntley's place tucked into the pockets of the violin case. If that were found.... Well, it would guarantee that he would be taken before the Mayor of Hell! The man in the front seat turned his bland, cold-eyed smile upon Wentworth, leveled a gun while the one called Slick patted over Wentworth's person for guns. He found the cheap revolver and the heavy automatic, but the knife between his shoulder blades escaped detection.

"What do you think about it now, Slick?" asked the man in front.

Slick cursed filthily, hit Wentworth across the face. "How was I to know the son had anything on him, Curly?" he said thickly. He started to hit Wentworth again, but a glimpse into the cold depths of his eyes checked the hand in mid-blow. Slick flinched back and lifted a gun. "You lousy mug," he whispered. "You lousy mug."

Wentworth smiled thinly, battling with the fierce rise of his temper. The man called Curly laughed softly. After that, there was silence in the car except for the whisper of the engine and the soft hiss of snow against the glass.

In the silence, the close half-dark of the car, Wentworth sensed abruptly that Nita was, of all things, quietly happy! He glanced at her with the frank curiosity a stranger might be expected to exhibit, and though she did not look at him, there was an upward curve to her red lips, a brilliance in her masked eyes. It was as if she cried aloud that since her Dick was alive, nothing could go wrong.

It came to him with a sense of overwhelming surprise that he was regarded as dead. These men, everyone, believed him dead. The full significance of that had somehow never struck him. There no longer was any danger that he would be identified as the Spider. Underworld and police no longer sought out his secret trails. In short, if he would let dead ghosts lie, there no longer was any reason why he should not reach out for the happiness that for so long he had denied himself—and Nita!

When he had met Nita, his life was already pledged to

the service of humanity, the Spider had been a scourge of the Underworld for three full years. So he had fought against the love he knew could never reach culmination in marriage. What man could marry, have a home and children, when death and disgrace hung hourly over his head? No, he could not permit Nita to face such a possibility. He had told her that, long ago, when they found their love was stronger than the will to resist, had told her all his secret life in the hope that it might accomplish what his will had not. It had only drawn Nita closer to him, and they had fought the hard way together.

NOW, SUDDENLY, blindingly, all the vistas of possibility that he had long put behind him opened up. The past was dead, the Spider was dead and could never rise to destroy happiness. Why not? Why not burst from this car, strike down these men and flee with Nita to the future they both had earned many times over? True, he had no money, but he had small doubts that he could rise swiftly again.

Wentworth's eyes dropped to his knotted hands, his lips twisted in a slow, wry smile. He looked again at Nita's smiling lips, at the gayness of her eyes and the pang was like a knife turning in his breast. He sucked in a deep breath, held it for so long that his temples began to thump with suffocation, then he expelled it slowly, silently, and with it he blew away the selfish dreams which for a few moments had given him a vision of a happiness that was never to be.

"Listen, Curly," said Wentworth in his normal, cultured voice, "I'm from Chicago. I came here to see if I couldn't sign with the Mayor for the big clean-up here. I figured if I pulled my old violin gag, some grifter would try to collect protection dough and I'd get a chance to meet the Big Shot. How about putting me next?"

Curly remained quietly smiling, his cold eyes slanted along the barrel of the gun. "How about the Black Widow here? What's she got to do with you?"

Wentworth shrugged, leered in Nita's direction. "Maybe she likes my physique?"

Curly guffawed, an explosive monosyllabic sound. "Maybe," he agreed, "but it sure must have been good to make her stop the taxi and get out. She didn't give *me* no tumble and I'm a damned sight better than you."

Wentworth had thrown off the beggar's character and had taken on another. He still was not Wentworth. He was a smart and hard crook from the West.

"Maybe," he grunted, "but here's the real lowdown. It's the fiddle."

"The fiddle?"

"Sure," Wentworth nodded. "Remember this Spider guy used to fiddle sometimes? Least, he did in Chicago once. It's a cinch that's what it was."

Curly slapped the back of the seat. "By God, I believe you've hit it! And this dame thinks maybe you're fiddling a message or something."

WENTWORTH SHRUGGED, lounged back on the cushions. He was conscious of Slick's small, black eyes fixedly on his face. He had taken a big chance, drawing a parallel between himself and the Spider, but he had had to give some explanation of Nita's action. Best not give them time to think about it. Wentworth turned on Slick. "And listen, mug," he snarled, "I don't know why you took such a hate on me, but don't let it run away with your brains, see? Next time you make a pass at me, it'll be your last."

Slick snarled back, but it was obviously bravado. He was cowed. There was a different game to play with Curly, obviously leader of this small group.

"You're a smart egg for a New Yorker, Curly," Wentworth told him in the condescending manner of the Western crook. "Took you to see I was packing a gun. And my fiddling is pretty good cover at that."

Curly grinned. "I'm pretty smart in any part of the country. I saw through you easy."

"You sure did, but I fooled this dumb egg you call Slick."

"Sure, Slick's dumb."

Slick stirred uncomfortably. "Keep on now, keep on," he muttered. "I'll get back at you."

"Back is right," Wentworth sneered at him, "It will have to be in the back. You haven't got the guts…."

Slick jerked up the gun to strike and Curly barked at him. "Cut it, Slick. And listen, mug, layoff him, see?"

Wentworth glowered at Slick. "No punk is going to slam me and get away with it."

"Who's a punk?" Slick lashed out with the gun. Wentworth pinned the gun and hand to the ceiling of the car and crossed his right to the jaw. Slick collapsed in the corner and Wentworth jerked up his hands, shoulder high.

"Don't shoot, Curly," he said, anxiously. "You know Slick had it coming to him."

He was just in time, Curly's face had lost its smile and his eye was cold behind the gun. "Maybe he did," Curly grunted, "but you hold your ears the rest of the way."

Wentworth nodded, grinning cheerfully. "Sure, it's all right now, but I had to pay that punk off."

Wentworth was thinking how easy it would be to whip a hand over his shoulder to the knife between his shoulder blades, its hilt just out of sight beneath his coat collar. Curly would die in a split-sec-

"Come one, come all," he chanted. "The Cross of Corporal Death shall reward you!"

ond and after that, the driver would be easy. The hilt of the knife, or the point, just beneath the ear. For a moment, Wentworth trembled on the brink of striking. How could he know what lay ahead? Suppose the Mayor, if finally he faced him, penetrated his trickery? He and Nita would both be doomed. Wouldn't it be better to get free now, take a chance on forcing information from Slick or the driver? But Wentworth played his cards the bolder way.

WENTWORTH STARED ahead through the thick, slanting haze of snow flakes. The car moved almost silently on white streets and the headlights threw ahead a diffused brilliance. He caught a glimpse of a high statue on his left. The car swung in a wide circle to the right, Central Park, West. Soon the sedan swerved to the left hand curb. Slick was still unconscious and the driver hauled him out, massaged his neck until he recovered enough to hold a gun shakily. Slick's eyes were murderous.

They went into an elaborate foyer, Curly beside Nita, the other two men with hidden guns in Wentworth's back, and up a private elevator for a considerable distance. When they left the cage, they stood in an elaborate reception room, all Oriental carpets and soft divans, crimson-shaded lights in execrable taste. It was so badly done that Wentworth felt instinctively that the whole thing was camouflage. Some person of excellent taste wished it to appear that he was otherwise….

There were a half-dozen men lounging about the reception room and they came swiftly, competently to their feet. None drew a gun, but Wentworth felt that weapons could fly to their hands with ominous quickness.

"Slick, go tell the big shot," Curly ordered shortly. Slick left reluctantly, his venomous eyes slitting sideways at Wentworth. Curly's laughter, behind Wentworth, was soft. "I'm afraid he don't like you anymore."

"I don't mind a punk like that," Wentworth said scornfully, "but I'd hate to have *you* down on me."

In the anteroom of the Big Shot, Curly grew cautious. "Listen, mug, I'm no pal of yours."

"Sure, not," Wentworth agreed cheerfully, "but after I talk to the Big Shot you will be."

Slick had vanished through a slide door that moved heavily. Now he came back, his black eyes returning to Wentworth's face. There was a hint of a crooked smile on the man's slit mouth.

A jab in the back sent Wentworth forward and he frowned in sharp surprise at the room they entered through the thick slide door. There wasn't a piece of furniture in it. Walls and floor were dead white and, the instant he crossed the threshold, dazzling lights flooded it from all sides. It was impossible to make out anything definite about the big-shouldered man who stood behind a curtain of light at the far end. Wentworth saw then that the three gunmen who held him and Nita prisoner had put on colored glasses.

Wentworth frowned his eyebrows low over his eyes, but could not see clearly. It was a clever device, the same that was used by police in the line-up, of focusing strong lights upon prisoners so that they could be seen clearly, but could see nothing of their observers.

The voice that spoke presently, coming from the man behind

the lights, was slow and melodious, a confirmation of Wentworth's guess that the bad taste displayed outside was pure camouflage.

"You claim to be from Chicago. Your name and connections, please?"

WENTWORTH WAS conscious that the men about him were tense with some emotion he could not fathom. Nita was beside him, thrust forward by Curly. She stood so close that their arms almost touched. Wentworth felt an almost irresistible desire to clasp her hand in his, to reassure her.

Wentworth grinned thinly into the white lights. "I don't like to talk to men I can't see," he said shortly. "How about telling *your* name and connections, as you put it?"

Nita's arm brushed his and joy leaped through him. That was approbation and he knew it. Nita had faced these lights before, of that he was suddenly positive. Curly's breath, hissing in between his teeth, made audible sound. Behind the lights was silence for seconds. The man's voice was calm and melodious as before.

"You asked to see the Mayor of Hell. You are in his Excellency's presence. Kindly refrain from putting on a show for the lady's benefit."

It was cleverly done. Wentworth had to acknowledge that. No bluster, no threatening—just a quietly sarcastic reprimand. It would have disconcerted the crook Wentworth was supposed to be, so he shuffled his feet and was slightly apologetic when he spoke. "I'm not showing off, but I'm not spilling anything until I know the guy I'm talking to. You say you're the Mayor, but that isn't proving it. I could say I was President Roosevelt, but that wouldn't make it so. Mister, there's money on my head and I've got to play it safe."

There was the same pause as before. "You are safe as long as I decree it. When I lift my protection, you die. Speak at once."

Wentworth shrugged. "Okay. I'm Biff Carmichael. I don't have connections because I go it alone. Only reason I made a play for you was I understand you got things sewed up so tight it's not safe to try anything might be called muscling in."

Biff Carmichael was well known. Two months ago, the Spider had killed him, and his appearance would roughly fit his own.

"Biff Carmichael is dead," the statement was without excitement, almost as if the man recited a lesson.

Wentworth grinned suddenly, happily. "That's what everybody thinks. The Spider got on my tail and killed a guy I'd planted to make him think it was me. I let it rest like that and didn't dare move until the Spider got his. You bumping him was what brought me into your camp. Any guy that can get the best of that one, I'm strong for." Admiration gleamed from Wentworth's face. "I'd like like hell to work for you—for a consideration."

"Play the violin," said the Mayor.

Wentworth put surprise on his face. He was filled with misgiving. There was something going all here that he did not understand. He had chosen Biff Carmichael because it was notorious that very few knew anything about him at all, such as whether or not he played the violin. He shrugged, looked around and Slick handed him the violin case. Wentworth laid it on the floor, crouched beside it. Was it possible that the Mayor was some man who had heard Richard Wentworth play? He had given a few private concerts for friends and acquaintances. Before this, he had found that criminal genius might mark out one of the social classes as well as the substrata. He would have to disguise his technique—no easy matter—for no man realizes what makes up his artistry. He uses certain mannerisms instinctively as a result of long practice.

There was a cold heart behind the slightly puzzled frown with which he lifted violin and bow from the case. He did not rosin the bow. Impossible to do that without opening a compartment in which he had stuffed money stolen from Huntley's home…. **HE STOOD** facing the lights, violin and bow held casually. He realized abruptly that the manner in which he held it, fingers delicate upon the strings, the chin rest against his hip, was characteristic of him. He gestured widely with the bow to distract attention, tucked the violin beneath his chin.

"What would you like to hear?" he queried. "I'll have to confess that my repertory is somewhat limited…."

"The Devil's Trill," the Mayor interrupted.

Wentworth laughed, "Sorry, don't know that one." He did and there was a coldness creeping up along his spine, seeming to center about that knife sheath against his backbone. That was a piece he always played. Not beautiful, but extremely difficult of technique, a thing that no one but a practiced musician would attempt, and an extraordinarily gifted virtuoso at that. The choice seemed to confirm his fear that the man had pierced his slight disguise….

"The Londonderry Air," came the next calm request.

That one Wentworth could not refuse. It had been that melody which he had played for Nita there where the snow swirled on Times Square.

The Mayor's voice broke into the music. "I think you need a bit of rosin, maestro."

The meaning was obvious. The Mayor had noticed that he failed to rosin his bow before playing. The Mayor suspected that there was a reason for not opening the compartment in which the money was hidden. Wentworth shrugged.

"A gift for you, Mayor," he said sardonically. He flipped open the rosin compartment and drew out tightly packed sheafs of currency. He heard Curly gasp. Slick took the money at an order and went with it through the veil of light. The back of Nita's hand was touching his and he could feel the quiver of a tendon as she moved a finger, concealed within her half-closed hand. The rhythm was unmistakable. Shorthand code. Dot-dash-dot; dot-dash….

"Gun in my right pocket," Nita's signals said swiftly, then her hand swayed clear of his. Evidently Nita knew something that he had missed. She was sure that it would come to a pitched battle….

Slick stepped clear of the veil of light, and the deep, musical voice came gently.

"I have heard of paying the fiddler," said the Mayor, "but I am quite sure I didn't pay you… nor did Alderman Huntley. Yet this is his money. Is it possible that you are… *Corporal Death?*"

## CHAPTER 8
## THE FIDDLER IS PAID

WENTWORTH'S KEEN mind leaped instantly to the solution of what was apparently magic on the part of the Mayor. The money had been given to Huntley by the Mayor and he had some means of identifying it. The fact that Wentworth had the bills in his possession, coupled him with the death of Huntley, indicated he was… Corporal Death!

Yet it had taken quick thinking to piece together the evidence so quickly. Wentworth's thoughts flew even more swiftly. Scarcely had the word "Corporal" left the lips of the man behind the lights when Wentworth was in action. His right hand whipped the violin bow violently about behind him, caught Curly across the face. The violin itself, he hurled straight at the dim figure behind the lights. In the continuation of the movements which had thrown the two missiles, his hands swept into action. His left snatched the gun from Nita's pocket. His right whipped the knife from between his shoulder-blades, and, in the same instant, he went headlong through the veil of light.

The light was a thin protection, but it would make shooting difficult for the gunmen. And he had business with the dim figure owning the melodious voice. His knife blade swept viciously through the air before his eye had become accustomed to the dimness and the voice was no longer musical. It keened terribly to a bitterly high pitch. Wentworth sliced again with the knife, then drove it violently forward, felt the blade bite deep. The screaming stopped and Wentworth dropped on his knees close against the wall with Nita's tiny automatic in his fist. It was a twenty-five caliber weapon, but of a good make. It was hard-shooting, accurate. If a man placed his bullets well, it would do as much damage as a forty-five. It would kill.

Peering through the veil of light from the dark side of the room, he saw that Nita had hurled herself to the floor, that the three men were charging forward with guns in their hands. They had been afraid to shoot through the light, for fear of hitting the Mayor, but they were already almost upon him. The sliding door across the blazing room was wrenched back and the men who had been on guard outside came charging through. Wentworth shot Slick first, putting the tiny pellet of lead between his eyes. Slick kept coming for three paces, then he smashed down dead on the floor. Wentworth laughed, flat, sinister, mocking.

"Come one, come all," he chanted softly. *"The Cross of Corporal Death shall reward you!"*

He fired again, dropped a man who was striding with a white, furious face toward Nita. The man's heavy gun crashed to the floor and Nita caught it up. Seven men left, seven men against a pop-gun and Nita's new weapon. Wentworth fired again, laughing, and—the lights went out.

Even the man who had extinguished the lights—who knew what was about to happen—did not move more swiftly than Wentworth. Knife in his left hand, the pop-gun in his right, he sped soft-footed across the floor to Nita's side. At his whisper, she moved with him back toward the body of the Mayor. They would not expect him to remain there, in the spot where they had last seen him.

Curly's voice rang out through the darkness: "Joe, guard the door. Don't let anybody out. The rest of you, backs against the wall where the door is. Come on, backs…."

His plan was obvious. An impenetrable line across the room, then a slow advance to the kill. Wentworth whipped off his cap; traded the twenty-five for Nita's heavier gun, buried its muzzle in the crown. When Curly shouted again, he fired. There was no flash. The crashing discharge filled the room and gave no sense of direction. Curly's voice choked off….

"Six left," Wentworth's thoughts ran. Six men with guns, anyone of whom could account for both Wentworth and Nita. Undoubtedly, there were more men of the Mayor of Hell somewhere about. But Wentworth found a rising exultation. He had killed the Mayor of Hell. It was ridiculously easy. He could scarcely believe the thing had been done, but he had felt the knife bite home and the man had screamed beneath the Cross of Corporal Death….

NITA'S SHOULDER was against his. He could feel the tenseness of her arm and knew that she held the twenty-five ready for instantaneous use. Six against these two, more strength coming for the six. Yes, he had killed the Mayor, but it seemed that the Corporal would greet the real Death this night. And Nita—darling, brave Nita of the violet eyes and the sweet smile—would go with him to that grisly appointment. Wentworth embedded the point of his knife in the floor at his feet and put his left arm about her shoulders. He drew her close, felt her breath warm and sweet against his cheek as she turned her mouth to his. She knew without words that this was goodbye.

Not that her Dick would give up without an effort… Their lips clung….

Wentworth's fingers pulsed out a quick message in swift Morse upon her wrist. He was going forward, toward the man in the door, would kill him silently if he could. He would go to the man at the remote right-hand end of the line they were forming and would kill him noisily. When that happened, she was to creep to the door. He would not be far behind her. Optimism that last. Lying, Nita thought. He would try to join her, yes, but with the odds even reduced to four to one, if he were successful both times in the darkness, what chance did he have?

It took time to press out that message in silent code, and the gunmen began to whisper one to another, to carry out the plan that Curly had laid before he died.

"No lights," whispered one, "this Corporal Death shoots like the Devil himself."

"No lights. All forward together. Shoot if you touch anything ahead."

"Ready?"

Wentworth squeezed Nita's arm and slid forward, silently, standing straight up as they would not expect him to do. They would shoot if they touched anything ahead. Wentworth's knife was ready, point forward. If any man touched him, that man was dead! Straight toward the door, Wentworth moved. Directly ahead of him, he heard a man's breathing, hoarse and shallow in his throat. Frightening business, this fighting in the dark. Wentworth's lips were thin with mockery. Well, the darkness was their own weapon. They had not thought it would prove two-edged!

A voice boomed out somewhere up toward the ceiling, a deep, harsh voice full of power:

"Fools! Turn on the light before he kills you all!"

Not five feet ahead of Wentworth, a man drew in a shaky, frightened breath. Wentworth took one long, soft stride ahead and the knife struck upward savagely. The throat, beneath the chin, was Wentworth's mark. If he miscalculated distance… He did—and hit the body low down. There was a gush of warm liquid and a man screamed in shuddering horror and dread. He could not know pain yet. He flopped, scrambling, to the floor, and Wentworth leaped wide to the right, the knife before him.

In the darkness, his face was twisted and white. Hell, a knife was not his kind of weapon. But it killed silently and swiftly and other men knew a terror of it which was greater than their fear of guns. His lips writhed in silent curses. He collided, flat-bodied, against a man in the darkness. The man screamed before the point of the knife slid between his ribs.

"The knife! *Good God, the knife!*"

"Lights, fools!" the voice boomed again.

Who could be shouting those wise orders? Wentworth frowned as he turned from his second kill toward the door. He had fought too often in the dark not to realize the importance of orientation. He moved unerringly through the thick blackness. He guessed that the light-switch was there somewhere. Men were in utter panic, screaming, banging against walls.

WENTWORTH'S HEART was tight with dread. Had Nita obeyed his orders and slipped to the door at the first outcry? If she had, she should be near him now.

"Nita," he risked a whisper amid the bedlam

"Dick!" Nita's hand found his arm.

It was at that instant that the lights blazed high and bright. Wentworth reached the door in a long stride, throwing a single glance over the room behind him, at the shambles his strategy had created. That booming voice worried him. It came from no man in the room. Its quality and its intelligence argued a leader of some sort, and its source indicated there had been a hidden observer of all that went on within the room. Was it possible that he had not killed the Mayor, but a puppet who spoke for him? Such things had happened before in the Spider's experience. If that were true, his life was forfeit a hundred times over and darling Nita....

He slammed shut the sliding door, found nothing to secure it, and flashed a glance about the room. The crimson lights still shed their bloody rays over everything, a vague illumination at best. He made out another door in a side wall and even as he spotted it, it flung open and men with guns rushed through. Wentworth flung Nita behind a heavily stuffed davenport and went down on his knees himself. His gun convulsed in his hand. He had six shots, he calculated. He fired with the calm, regular efficiency of the target range. The men were crowding in the doorway and he took them in swift, even sequence. When the gun was empty....

Nita pressed her own small automatic into his left hand. He tried to count back—to figure the number of bullets left in that—but the action was too swift. One of the men had caught up the falling body of a companion and was walking forward with it, firing as he came. A bullet drifted white plaster dust down over Wentworth's head. Damn it, this man would take two bullets to stop, two bullets he could not spare. He shot the man's legs and as he pitched downward, put a second bullet through the top of his head.

He dropped the empty gun, snapped three quick shots with the pop-gun and the third clicked on an empty chamber. There were still men in that choked doorway. One of those who had fallen to the floor was not dead and his gun began to sound. Behind the davenport, Wentworth dared a quick glance toward Nita and met a smile. She was fumbling a fresh clip into the little automatic, but even she knew that it would be too late. Men were opening the sliding door behind them. Seconds now, short seconds…. Wentworth saw that the elevator indicator above the door was swinging over. More reinforcements for the Mayor of Hell. Damn it, he would not give up. He reached for the cord of one of the crimson lamps. He could short-circuit it, give them darkness to fight in. He might get a gun from a dead man….

"That wasn't the Mayor you killed," Nita said swiftly. "We must get out."

The elevator door clashed open and Wentworth, with his knife blade against the lamp cord, hesitated, then sent his laughter like a challenge. The doorway of the elevator showed only three persons, three persons with knives gripped between their teeth, and guns in their hands, and one of them sprayed bullets from a sub-machine gun like water from the nozzle of a hose. That was Len Roberts, and on each side of him, automatics kicking in their hands, were the O'Rourkes, father and daughter!

WITH A shout, Wentworth sprang from behind the davenport and snatched up guns. He pivoted, blazed at the opening doorway behind him and drove a hail of bullets into the midst of the men there.

"The scourge of Corporal Death!" he shouted.

It was over in less than a minute after the sub-machine gun had begun to spit its leaden hail. Kathleen O'Rourke came forward at a run. She was staggering on her feet, her face white and working. "Come!" she choked. "The police will be here any minute."

Wentworth whirled toward Nita and a cry like a curse rose in his throat. She was unconscious on the floor and there was blood upon her dress. Wentworth snatched her up. For a space of seconds, he stood there with his sweetheart in his arms, his face stricken. Then he staggered toward the elevator. He heard a gun crash out, then another in quick succession. Pat O'Rourke was hanging onto the wall of the elevator with a clawing hand. It was his gun that had spoken last, and it was plain he had taken the lead meant for Wentworth's back.

Len Roberts leaped backward into the cage; Kathleen threw the lever and they plummeted downward.

"Pop, Pop!" she sobbed. "Is it bad? Oh, Pop, is it…?"

"Those dirty spalpeens aren't after killing me yet," O'Rourke gasped. His forehead was beaded with sweat. "A bit of a crease across my ribs."

Wentworth scarcely heard them, gazing down into the still white face of Nita. Corporal Death had won a victory—but at what a fearful cost! He scarcely heard Kathleen as she explained

87

that she had followed when he had bidden her remain at home, that she had chosen to pursue him rather than her father and Len Roberts when they had separated. She had got to them barely in time after the men of the Mayor had carried him and Nita into the apartment house. They had killed with their knives at first, then seized guns…. Kathleen was sobbing when she explained. As they staggered across the lobby, she was violently sick, and when they reached the automobile which, Wentworth saw, was still that of Alderman Huntley, she could only sag wretchedly into the seat beside Len as he sent the black car skittering over snowy pavements. They left the wail of sirens swiftly behind.

They were free. Corporal Death could strike again, but the Mayor of Hell still lived, and God, oh God, what was the use of anything if Nita, his Nita…? With a choked sob, Wentworth bent his lips to her throat….

## CHAPTER 9
## DISASTER

PRESENTLY, THE big limousine drew to a halt and Len Roberts strode away to return in a few minutes, alone, in a taxicab. Wentworth transferred numbly to the other machine. He had examined Nita's wound. It was severe, high through the chest, near the joints of the collar bone. There was a thread of blood at the mouth corner which meant the lung was punctured. Not necessarily a fatal wound, but she must have expert medical attention, and quickly.

When finally the taxi drew to a halt near the tenement home of the O'Rourkes, Wentworth took the wheel.

"I'm taking the lady to a doctor," he said shortly. "She's in a bad way and she gave me a break back there in the fight. Go home and I'll join you."

Len Roberts looked at him intently. "Better take Pat, too. He's got it bad in the side."

"Sure, hop in, Pat," Wentworth said.

O'Rourke growled. "A scratch. Bounced off my rib. I'll doctor it myself."

Wentworth nodded, sent the cab forward. The tires skidded, then creaked on the thick white snow. It had stopped falling and the cleaning crews already were at work. A streetcar plow whirled past, throwing up a thick haze of white moisture. Wentworth doubled uptown, stopped on Fifth Avenue, then caught up Nita in his arms and staggered around the corner. The snow was to the calf of his legs and untrampled. He was leaving a plain trail that he would have to destroy after he had taken care of Nita.

The doctor's butler, grotesque in an oversize dressing-gown, staggered back at the point of a gun. When the doctor came grimly downstairs, his mouth was set in a tight-lipped line, his wiry red hair stood on end, but when his eyes found Nita's face, his whole body jerked in surprise.

"Good God!" he cried. "Nita van Sloan."

He stared keenly at Wentworth as he threw open a door, jerked an order to the butler.

"Listen," Wentworth said roughly. "The cops're on my tail

an' I gotta beat it. The dame gave me a break in a shoot-up an' I promised to get her to a doc. She said come here. Is it all right?"

The doctor nodded shortly. "It's all right. Now get out of here. I've already telephoned the police."

Wentworth hesitated, staring down at Nita's white face, the dark shadows of her eyes beneath the lids. As he looked, Nita's lids fluttered and she muttered something, a name, his own.

"Get out!" the doctor snapped again. "I'll take care of her. Is she in danger from the police?"

"Maybe," Wentworth told him. "The cops're all crooks nowadays. She was kidnapped by a crook that's pals with the police, an' we shot our way out. You figure it out." He backed toward the door. His face twisted uncontrollably. "Take good care of her, doctor." And Wentworth was gone, out through the hallway, into the snow. He ran along the trail he had made carrying Nita, kicking it, destroying it all the way to the cab. He sprang into it and raced away.

He abandoned the taxi finally for a subway and sat, head down, lurching to the noisy, rough sway of the train as it rumbled downtown. A heavy weariness pulled at his whole body, made his limbs leaden. There was an ache in his back from his wounds and pain throbbed through his right arm. A strenuous night for a man so recently near the portals of death. A partial victory had been won, but it was without elation that Wentworth reviewed it. Dr. Higgins would take care of Nita all right. Wentworth had done him a service once that Higgins could never forget, and besides, his fees were ample. Yes, Higgins would take care of Nita. Pat O'Rourke....

ABRUPTLY, WENTWORTH snapped erect in his seat. Why, damn it, neither the O'Rourkes, nor Len Roberts, had worn a mask when they crashed into the Mayor's stronghold, and there had been live men left behind. It was just possible that some of them had known Patrolman Roberts… and Wentworth had told them to go home! He threw a sharp glance at the sign of a station when the train slowed, bolted for the door. He was aware abruptly that he was without efficient arms. The gun he carried had only three bullets in it and there were no spare cartridges.

The wind slapped him in the face with an icy hand as he broke from the subway stairs. It whipped tiny mists of snow from the dry powder that filled the streets and swept it along like miniature bullets. Wentworth's run was rapidly cut to a lumbering trot. His lungs pumped painfully. He drove on. Those loyal three, Len and Pat and his daughter, were in this solely because of his urging. They trusted to his leadership and he had been so blinded by Nita's need of him that he had sent them into what might be a death-trap!

Short of the last corner, Wentworth slowed and cringed close against the tenement wall. The snow caught the reflection of corner lights and brightened even the darkest streets, so that his black silhouette stood out strongly. There was frantic need for speed—yet to dash into the building would be madness. If police already had struck, they would have set up a plant to snare any other members of the group who should return later.…

Wentworth peered cautiously around the corner… and knew that his premonitions had been right. All along the street, the snow was smooth and white except for a few automobile tracks, but before the tenement there were a hundred foot marks, a half-dozen automobile paths. Even as Wentworth watched, two men in nondescript clothing began hurriedly to clear the walk of snow.

Through long seconds, Wentworth clung to the wall of the building, and the reaction of his strenuous exertions set in. His legs shook beneath him, there was a weakness in the small of his back so that he could scarcely stand. Had the police taken his allies away, or were they held in O'Rourke's rooms to trap other accomplices, himself? If his friends were there, it was his fault and he must free them. Wentworth retraced his steps until he reached a building on the opposite side of the block from O'Rourke's house, then he went into the dark doorway. There was a man in a torn overcoat curled up on the floor asleep, a Bowery bum... But was it? Wentworth opened the inner door and in the added light glimpsed a smooth-shaven cheek, a young, firm chin.

Wentworth's automatic flashed to his hand and the man on the floor galvanized into action. He sat up, reaching for a gun-butt plainly visible now in the waistband of his trousers. He was seconds too slow. Wentworth's automatic bumped against his skull and the man lay down again. Beneath the torn overcoat, Wentworth saw that he wore police uniform trousers. He handcuffed the man with his own shackles to the banister of the stairs inside, then with the cop's cap on his head, walked on through the sour, cold hallway to the court behind the building. There would be more police on watch here. Wentworth stood so that the light behind him made him clearly visible and hissed between his teeth.

"Come here, quick," he whispered into the darkness. "Gang out front." He ducked back into the hallway then, crouched in shadows which hid him completely. For seconds, nothing at all happened. Then a figure in police uniform flitted silently into the doorway.

"Hist! Bill!" he whispered.

"Here," called Wentworth, in the same tone. "They're out front, and…."

THE COP came within reach and Wentworth struck with sharp efficiency, his stiffened fingers gouging into throat nerves that spilled the man, instantly unconscious, to the floor. Wentworth took his gun, and extra bullets to add to those of the cop out front. Both of the revolvers were light-framed Police Positives, not an easy gun to hold on a target, but hard-hitting and deadly.

Wentworth had scarcely hidden the unconscious man in the shadows when a second policeman showed in the doorway. He stood on braced legs with his gun in his fist, his sharp eyes darting about the hallway. Abruptly, he leveled the gun toward the shadows where Wentworth stood.

"Come out of there," he ordered harshly.

Wentworth came out, but not in the way the policeman had intended. In the darkness, he whipped out the long-bladed Bowie knife and it whistled through the air ahead of his charge. Its keen point sliced through the man's arm, pinned it against the wall and, as the gun dropped from nerveless fingers, Wentworth's stiffened fingers once more performed their task and the policeman fell.

A swift, examination showed that no artery had been cut in the man's arm, and Wentworth sped out into the darkness of the court. There was no further interruption to his swift progress. He labored over a fence, reached the back of O'Rourke's tenement, slipped into the hall.

In front of the building, he could hear the rasp of shovels as the two men went hurriedly about cleaning the sidewalk. Would there be other guards in front? Wentworth made no sound as he stole toward the stairs. Not a board creaked under his stealthy feet and he sped up the steps. The O'Rourkes were on the third floor, a railroad flat that began at the head of the steps and ran back to the rear. There was no means of entrance except the front door. Just before his head reached the level of the third floor, Wentworth stopped, stretched out full length on the steps, and slid upward until he could look about. The hall gas-jet was turned unusually high, but no door slit showed light.

Wentworth lay frowning, listened intently. And then he heard it; heard a woman gasp out a sob, heard her pleading. It was there in the tones, though he could hear no words. Once she screamed, a sound that was quickly muffled. And he knew the voice, Kathleen's!

It might be a trap, but Wentworth could not delay to wonder about that. If it were Kathleen who cried out like that, she was in need of help, and terribly so. Wentworth was beside the door of the O'Rourke apartment in quick strides, twisting the knob. It would be unlocked, of course, so that the prey could enter the trap more readily. Wentworth counted on that. He twisted the knob and went through in a single, swift rush of action; went bounding across the room, toward the portieres on the opposite side which showed a thread of light between them.

THERE WAS a startled curse, then Wentworth whipped aside the curtains. A man had been standing with his back toward the draperies and he had only twisted half-about, reaching for his gun. Wentworth slapped him with the barrel of a ready revolver, but there was no such gentle treatment for the other two men in the room. They were both fat-padded huskies of the Strong-Arm Squad, beef-faced maulers picked for that precise purpose. One was lounging at ease in a big chair. The other had Kathleen in his arms. Her smooth golden hair was tumbled in wild disorder. Her face was livid and red in welts where she had been slapped again and again and the strength was almost gone from her. Her dress hung in tatters from naked shoulders.

Wentworth took in the picture in a single swift flicker of his cold eyes. The two men had whipped surprised faces about, the one in the chair was crouched forward, half out of it, dragging at a revolver in his hip pocket; the other made a clumsy attempt to swing Kathleen about as a shield. The knife of Corporal Death was too swift.

The man's scream died still-born. His arms sagged from about Kathleen and the two bounded apart as if from collision. The policeman wavered on his feet and the second man in the chair got his gun free from the holster, started it around his body. Wentworth laughed at him, leaped forward, jabbed his revolver against the man's belly and pulled the trigger. The shot didn't make much noise.

Wentworth was looking into the face of the second policeman as he shot him. He saw the dark blood rush into his fat cheeks, inject his widening eyes as the punch of lead hurled him deep back into the chair, saw the eyes roll up as a bloody cough robbed him of consciousness. Wentworth moved back slowly, three short steps and stood gazing at him. The cop wasn't dead yet, wouldn't die for a while that would be full of agony. But he'd die too soon at that.

Kathleen, when he turned, was crouched against the wall. Her hands were over her face and sobs wrenched at her bare shoulders. Wentworth looked at her strangely. The Spider, for all his fierce warfare, had never before killed a policeman. These two deserved death, God knew, but it was strange nevertheless that she should have been the cause of it. Wentworth's eyes, focusing on the man who had died of his knife, became round and hard. He bent over and put his foot against the man's cheek as he dragged loose the wedged knife.

"That shot didn't make much noise," he said shortly, "but we'd better get out of here."

The girl's hands came down. Her eyes were dry, but her shoulders still shook. Wentworth helped her to her feet, gave her a coat from the cretonne-covered racks in a corner and she was still sobbing as he led her from the place, where the Cross of Corporal Death marked his dead. He left her in the hallway and returned, went swiftly through the pockets of the three men. They were singularly well-lined for policemen....

Wentworth left the tenement by the same course he had used on entering. None of the policemen he had felled was yet conscious. In the cold air, Kathleen ceased her sobbing, but she did not speak until he had found rooms for them both in a shoddy hotel. She glared at him there, her fists white and knotted at her sides.

"You did very well when you came," she said harshly, "but you're a bit too late. They shot Pop twice when he didn't have a gun in his hand, then broke Len's leg with a bullet. They'd have killed them both if… if I hadn't promised to stay behind with… with them. And it's your fault. *Your fault!* Just because Pop felt sorry for you, and… and…."

Kathleen bowed her face into her hands and the crazy sobs burst from her again. Wentworth stood, saying nothing, hands hanging limply at his sides. There was self-mockery on his face. Victor, was he? For a few hours, he had seemed to triumph, but now he was alone again, stripped of all help, his friends, his sweetheart shot down, even this girl alienated. He turned sharply away from her, strode to the door. By God, he would not be beaten! Somewhere, somehow he would find the Mayor of Hell, and then…!

## CHAPTER 10
## A STRANGE MEETING

WENTWORTH STARTED toward his own room, but changed his mind and went hurriedly to the lobby. He must have rest, the more so since his body was drained by his recovery from near-death, but he dared not rest where Kathleen could find him. She was bitter now and she might, in a moment of hatred, betray him to the police. To her mind, it might be justice…. He got stationery, wrote a brief note urging her to remain at the hotel and promising to liberate her lover and father when they should be strong enough. He enclosed a share of the money he had taken from the police and left the letter in charge of the clerk for her. Afterward, he went swiftly out into the bitter December dawn. He ate rapidly in an all-night restaurant, made his way to another middle-class hotel and soon flung himself down to sleep.

It was late afternoon when he awoke and he sent out for newspapers, ordered a meal brought to his room. He bathed and, with a grimace of distaste, put the same clothing on again. He felt shoddy, ill-kempt. Jenkyns would have shuddered in horror at the idea. Wentworth wondered what had become of his loyal butler. He knew that Jenkyns had saved plenty to satisfy him for the rest of his life, even though he received nothing from the estate of his master. Sitting by the window, staring out at the snow which the city's smoke had already made filthy, Wentworth knew a feeling of utter unreality. Was it actually possible that he had been ripped from all that he held dear? He laughed shortly at himself, glanced down at his soiled cuffs and shot them back into his coat sleeves….

His breakfast came, the afternoon newspapers. The shooting on Central Park West, in the headquarters of the Mayor of Hell, was called a "gang massacre," and police were hunting for a man who called himself Corporal Death and who marked his victims with a knife. The murder of Alderman Huntley was headlined, and once more there was a mention of Corporal Death, together with a garbled description. Police and newspapers shouted demands for the capture of the "fiend who called himself Corporal Death."

Two of the "fiend's" associates had been captured, the papers went on, and were being guarded against demands for a lynching. A woman, Kathleen, was described as a red-headed gun moll—had escaped with the help of her paramour, Corporal Death, who had killed two police. Yes, they were shouting for his blood. Well, Wentworth smiled grimly as he set about eating, newspapers and police had screamed for the blood of the Spider before this and he still lived. The shrieking did not bother him. To an extent it helped.

Wentworth forced himself to finish the meal, but already impatience was burning within him. He had no clues—no hint of where next to form contact with the men of the Mayor of Hell—but there was one obvious point of attack: Senator Hoey! It was so obvious that Wentworth knew the man would be guarded by an impenetrable ring of defenses which he must nevertheless pierce. Wentworth stared at the picture of the Senator, displayed across three columns on the front page of the newspaper. His curly head was lifted high and his bulging jowls fairly quivered with the indignation of his demand that the police avenge his dear friend Huntley. Wentworth laughed shortly, unpleasantly. Through that utterance, he could feel Hoey's dread that the same fate awaited him. Yes, by all means, avenge Huntley and rid Hoey's sleep of dreams of the Cross of Corporal Death!

There was no mention in the newspapers of Nita van Sloan, nor of Doctor Higgins, but Wentworth feared to make a call from the hotel to learn his sweetheart's condition. He finished his toilet, left the hotel unobtrusively and, from a corner drugstore, phoned Higgins. The doctor was curt.

"Clean wound," he said. "Considerable hemorrhage but she has a chance to recover if there are no complications. Don't call here again. You involved me more than sufficiently with the police last night."

HIGGINS' HANG-UP was explosive and Wentworth was grave as he left the booth and made his way to a florist shop, directed that two dozen American Beauties be delivered to Higgins' home "for his special patient." Attached to the blank card which he fastened to the roses was only a single, blue corn flower, but it would be sufficient. Nita would know that signature of the flower he always wore on his evening-dress lapel. When that was done, he examined his money and grimaced in surprise. Richard Wentworth was not used to economy and his funds were running dangerously low. Still he would have to afford one thing, cartridges for his revolvers. And at the first opportunity, he would have to pay a visit to another of Hoey's henchmen to bolster his finances.

He referred again to the newspaper in his pocket, saw that Senator Hoey was at the Mayfair and, after buying bullets, Wentworth made his way uptown on the clanking, slow, elevated train. The early winter dusk was already closing in upon the icy-streeted city and advertising lights blossomed crimson and blue and white. The slattern tenements and jumbled, dusty-windowed shops were draped in twilight, their scars and lumpy figures built into shadowy curves. Poetry here for a man who loved the city and Wentworth, gazing out upon it, felt emotion close his throat. There was hunger and privation here, side by side with luxury; there was crime and all things vile, but also aspiration and the mead of success, each man according to his desserts.

Wentworth beheld his city as a cross-section of all the cities of the world, even as it was the queen of them all. People, striving for happiness, finding their burdens made greater, even their meager share of life cramped and laced with tragedy because one man—one group of men—was drunk with power. The thought of the Mayor of Hell robbed the dusk of beauty, turned the night into a furtive shield for criminals.

Anger drove poetry from Wentworth's soul. He got abruptly to his feet, lurched from the train. A few blocks away stood the Mayfair Hotel and there was the man who was responsible for the rising tide of tragedy.

Wentworth attained the ante-room of Hoey's office without much trouble. Hoey made a great pretense of charitable works. A man seeking a job might see him personally and the room into which Wentworth was ushered contained a half-dozen such men as he seemed to be, rather shabbily clad, pinched by cold, and seeking help.

From a corner, farthest from the inner door, Wentworth slowly surveyed the faces of the men. He could sense tension in their bearing as if it were a tangible electricity. They sat too still, too stiffly, kept their eyes too persistently on the floor. Were they part of Hoey's defenses, additional guards placed there since the attack upon Huntley? Somehow, Wentworth did not believe they were. Two policemen stood on each side of the inner door and it was always a policeman who opened the door of Hoey's office. Two more had stood in the hall outside. Surely, these were enough. What, then, was the business of these men?

WENTWORTH HAD come to the office largely to spy out the arrangements for Hoey's protection, to discover means of ingress and escape so that later he might strike. Now he was overwhelmingly certain that someone was before him. Why else were all these men waiting so tensely? At least one of the door guards was suspicious, to judge from his watchful stare.

Wentworth got to his feet and shambled toward the guard, playing his part of a cringing petitioner.

"Can the Senator see me today?" he whined. "I don't want to have to wait a couple of hours and then be told to come back tomorrow. It ain't fair to do a man that way. There's lots of people ahead of me, and…."

"Stow it, stow it," the guard growled, putting a hand forcibly against Wentworth's chest. "If you don't want to wait, don't. It ain't the Senator wants to see *you*, you're the one wants to see *him*, see? You can wait, or not. Go sit down."

Wentworth shrank back from the hand, but he stayed close, still whining. He didn't know what was in the wind, but if it was hostile to Senator Hoey, he wanted to help.

"It ain't fair," Wentworth repeated. "Me, I've waited a thousand hours in lines the last year and they're always telling you go away and come again. And I...."

The outer door opened and Wentworth twisted his head about that way. "See there's somebody else, now, and he'll have to wait...."

Wentworth had difficulty in forcing his voice to go on, for he knew that latest man to enter, knew him past any doubt, though he had shaved off the sharp military mustache he always wore and though there was an affected stoop in the usual erect confidence of his bearing. It was his friend, the former governor, Stanley Kirkpatrick! The guard gave Wentworth another shove and he stumbled away, glancing at the six waiting men. Their eyes were fixed on Kirkpatrick there by the door, watching him alertly.

Wentworth shuffled toward Kirkpatrick. "Don't you wait, buddy," he said shrilly. "It's a cheat! They ain't intending to let us in today, but just keep us waiting and waiting."

Kirkpatrick avoided him deftly, his saturnine face impassive, went straight toward the guard at the door. The man circled him, came after Wentworth with his head pulled down belligerently and Kirkpatrick faced the other guard. Wentworth's heart was pounding joyfully in his chest. He needed no word from Kirkpatrick to understand what was happening. Kirkpatrick had been ousted from office by unfair means. He had decided to fight the Mayor of Hell outside the law, as the Spider had done before him and these six men were here to help him kidnap Hoey.

Wentworth threw out his hands before him defensively, whining at the guard. "Now, you leave me alone," he said. "I've got rights. I'm an American citizen and you can't do me this way…!" Good God, wouldn't Kirkpatrick ever strike? The time was ideal, the guards separated where they could be bowled over quietly and at once. Ah! The six men were on their feet. The guard to whom Kirkpatrick was talking opened his mouth to cry a warning and Wentworth saw Kirkpatrick's shoulders rock, saw his whole body from heel to fist swing into a punch. Wentworth went into action in the same instant. The guard was reaching out for his collar to run him out of the office. Wentworth swayed in close and lanced out with stiff fingers. He caught the policeman as he slumped and eased him to the floor.…

KIRKPATRICK TURNED about, stared in amazement at the other policeman, laid on the floor, at the man crouched over him, but he had no time for inquiry. The attack he had begun must go through like lightning if it were to succeed.

"Bill! Jim!" he whispered. "Take out the two outside. The rest of you with me."

Two of the men moved to the outer door, opened it casually and went out grumbling. There was the scrape of feet on the floor, a grunt and a gasp and the two men returned dragging the two unconscious police. Wentworth bent over them, rapidly clasping their handcuffs on their wrists. The two called Bill and Jim assisted him. One of them grinned, his mouth opening in a wide smile.

"Don't know who you are, Buddy," he said, "but you sure know your stuff."

Wentworth kept his carping whine. "Ah, these Cossacks make me sore."

There were six men at the inner door now, behind Kirkpatrick. He motioned sharply to Wentworth, then without waiting for an answer whipped open the inner door and went in at a charge. Wentworth groaned. It was madness, suicide. He should have got in there by subterfuge, got a gun on the men inside before he called in his men. There was going to a gun battle....

Even as Wentworth started forward on a dead run, guns blasted out inside the office. One of Kirkpatrick's men reeled backward through the door, slumped forward on his knees. He braced himself with one hand and lifted a heavy revolver, began shooting. Wentworth was within two paces of him when the top leaped off of the man's head and the body shivered to the floor. Wentworth's guns were out now. He saw a man crouched behind a desk, sharp-shooting with his gun braced against the top. Wentworth fired from the hip and his bullet drove the man over sideways with a hole through his temple. Then Wentworth stepped into the inner office.

A door was closing across the room and a quick glance about showed that Senator Hoey had fled. There were five policemen still on their feet and as many more were stretched out on the floor. Why, damn it, Kirkpatrick had led his men into a murder trap! Kirkpatrick was down on one knee, with blood on his thigh. There were only two of his men still erect and even as Wentworth sprang into action, one of those took a bullet in the belly and folded slowly, agonizingly forward over clenching hands.

Wentworth used both revolvers from the hip, shooting them independently. He did not have to aim. From the first day he had donned the mantle of the Spider, he had realized that his life would frequently depend upon the accuracy of his fire and he had practiced with an intensity few men could equal. He had duplicated every feat of gun-fire ever recorded.

Wentworth's two guns blasted together and two policemen went down, already dead with their bullet-pierced hearts. One of the remaining three men turned toward Wentworth, his wide-open mouth shouting a warning, his revolver pivoting wildly. He and the man next to him went down together.

Wentworth had no need to fire again, for Kirkpatrick's bullets took care of the remaining policeman and Wentworth turned toward his friend. Kirkpatrick was pushing himself heavily to his feet on his wounded leg. The two men who had fought beside him lay motionless upon the floor. Kirkpatrick's face was awry with grief and defeat. Wentworth reached his side in long strides, threw a supporting arm about him.

Kirkpatrick seemed dazed and Wentworth saw there was a bullet crease, red and oozing blood, along the side of his skull. He went weakly where Wentworth led—toward the door through which Senator Hoey had escaped. Wentworth felt shaken and a little sick. He had shot at policemen—and shot to kill! Those brave blue uniforms with their seal of death in red upon their tunics rocked him as not even his first kill had stricken the Spider. But Kirkpatrick, who loved the police who had been his "boys" for so many years, had attacked them with gunfire. Wentworth's heart lifted a little. If Kirkpatrick had done that, he must have known past any doubt that these cops were crooks. Otherwise, nothing could have driven him to the murderous attack....

Wentworth reached the door and whipped it open. There were three more policemen, creeping toward the door with drawn revolvers in their hands...!

## CHAPTER 11
## ONE MAN'S DESPAIR

WENTWORTH HAD one advantage in his battle against death and that was surprise. The three police had expected to creep upon their prey and take them by surprise. They were soft-footing to the door when it whipped open and in that split-second of off-guard amazement, Wentworth had attacked. It was ever the Spider's way, the thing that had saved him in a thousand fights. It was not even, any longer, a matter of conscious thought but an instinctive reflex.

He dived headlong at the nearest man, the gun in his left hand blasted at a second policeman as he leaped. That was all there was time for before his shoulder caught the cop in the pit of the stomach. The man reached out pinioning arms as he went down with an agonized gasp for air. Getting free cost precious seconds. Wentworth struck with his revolver barrel at the man's head, rolled free, and tried to stagger to his feet. A heavy blow glanced with numbing pain on his head, hurled him to his face on the floor. A gun blasted almost in his ear. He rolled, firing upward blindly, caught a glimpse of a red, angry face and shot again.

For the first time since his attack, he saw the situation in the hall. The man he had slugged was flat on his back on the floor. The red-faced policeman was tottering on his feet, arms flung wide, gasping for air. Blood was beginning to stain the breast of his tunic. The third man, the one at whom Wentworth had fired when he dived, had his back against the wall and his revolver lifted high. He was bringing it down to shoot. His left arm hung limply. Wentworth had hit him, but not effectively. The man could hardly miss at this point-blank range. They were not ten feet apart and the gun was already descending. The cop's face was twisted, his eyes very wide, so that the whites showed. His hat sat crazily on his head with the visor over one ear.

Wentworth saw all those things as he whipped over his thirty-eight and pulled the trigger. The sound of the hammer, hitting on an empty chamber, was the loudest sound Wentworth had ever heard—and the most futile. There was no time to do more, no time even to move, for he had taken his last split-second of time, of his life, he realized, to snap the hammer of an empty gun.

The cop's revolver came down. Wentworth did not cease trying. He pushed up and to one side, heard an explosion like the crack of doom. Wentworth came to his feet with the momentum of his thrust, sprang forward to grapple with the cop. A wild cry was in his brain. "He missed me! He *missed* me!" He caught the cop's gun wrist, twisted it aside, drove his right fist in hard to the man's belly, rammed in with his shoulder.

The wrist was strangely limp in his fist; the weight against his shoulder.... Wentworth turned his head and stared at the cop's face, then he reeled backward with a gasp. The man's face had vanished and in its place was a bloody smear. That shot…? Wentworth pivoted toward Kirkpatrick. He was stretched out on his face, the revolver thrust ahead of him. He was unconscious now, but he had clung to his senses long enough—just long enough—to kill the policeman who was about to shoot Wentworth.

WENTWORTH GOT a revolver that held some cartridges in his right fist and stooped beside Kirkpatrick. It cracked his muscles, but he got his friend's body across his shoulders in a fireman's lift and staggered toward the door of the private elevator on which Hoey had escaped. There would be more police downstairs probably, reinforcements from headquarters, radio cars.… Wentworth calculated swiftly as he sent the cage downward. He knew how deceptive time spent in swift action could be. Perhaps three minutes, at the most, had passed since that first shot. Even if the alarm had gone through at the very onset of Kirkpatrick's attack, a radio car could scarcely have reached the scene yet.…

Wentworth groped open the door on the first floor, shoved his revolver into his pocket. A man in plain clothes came loping across the lobby with a pistol in his hand.

"For God's sake, get up there," Wentworth gasped at him. "We've got them holed up, but they're likely to crash out. I've got to get Hoey's secretary to a hospital quick."

The man hesitated, waited while Wentworth moved toward him. Wentworth reeled.

"Here, take him," he gasped and pushed Kirkpatrick's body

against the man's chest. He grabbed hold instinctively and Wentworth got out from under his load, got his gun pocket against the man's back.

"To the door," he rasped into the man's ear. "One word and I'll blow your backbone in half."

The man still had his gun in his hand, but his arm was under Kirkpatrick's shoulders. He would have to drop his burden before he could use that arm, and meantime, there was a gun muzzle against his spine. He went stumbling toward the door as an ambulance and radio car whirled up together.

"Hoey's office," Wentworth yelled at the cops. "Tried to kill us—half a dozen men. Got Hoey's secretary here...."

His gun muzzle rasped against his prisoner's backbone, kept him stumbling on toward the ambulance. The cops went toward the hotel door and another radio car whipped around the corner, just in time to see their companions dart through the doors.

"Tried to kill Hoey and us!" Wentworth yelled at them. "Six men up there, barricaded."

One of the cops went inside, the other came up to the ambulance where the interne was opening the doors.

"Who's that?" he demanded.

"Hoey's secretary," Wentworth told him swiftly, "He jumped in front of the Senator, and...."

Wentworth struck in the middle of the sentence, his left looping out like dynamite. The cop went down and Wentworth whipped out his revolver, sliced at the head of the man who had just deposited Kirkpatrick on the ambulance floor. He fell across the step and the interne, up inside with his hands under Kirkpatrick's shoulders, looked at him with his blue eyes popping behind tortoise-shell glasses. Wentworth motioned with the revolver.

"Inside, quick," he snapped. "Tell your driver to get away from here fast. This man has to get on the operating table…."

**THE DRIVER** had only a narrow pane of glass for rear vision. He could see nothing beyond the interne's back. Wentworth got on the step, holding the gun on the interne and the ambulance whipped away from the curbing and went screaming through the traffic. The interne dragged Kirkpatrick laboriously inside and Wentworth followed, shut the door.

"I don't want to slug you," Wentworth told the interne, "but I'm in a hurry, and…."

The interne backed toward the front of the ambulance. His face was pale, but his eyes had narrowed down. "Listen," he said, "I've seen what guns can do, both ways. You give the orders." He managed a shaky smile. Wentworth smiled back at him. The kid had nerve all right.

"I didn't notice what hospital," Wentworth said.

"Polyclinic," the interne said succinctly.

Wentworth frowned. That was on West Sixty-Second Street. He glanced out at the traffic, saw that they were cutting across Fifty-Ninth Street where chauffeured cars were fifty to the block. If he could pick a fast one… He knocked out the window behind the driver.

"See that Lincoln ahead?" he asked harshly. "Pin it to the curb."

The driver looked at the business end of the revolver and got the idea. The ambulance crowded in on the Lincoln and Wentworth motioned to the interne. "Get him on your shoulders. Come on, hurry."

The interne moved with strange alacrity, even grinning while he picked up Kirkpatrick. "I believe you really did try to bump Hoey," he said. "Sorry you missed."

Wentworth nodded toward Kirkpatrick. "He did. I'm just getting him out of a jam. I'm sorry he missed, too." He was frowning. Already, enemies were beginning to build up against Hoey, but it would avail nothing. They would never succeed against him at the crooked ballotings.

The interne put Kirkpatrick into the pinned Lincoln. A traffic policeman was pounding up the street, revolver in his hand. Wentworth swore. "Get that ambulance out of the way. Driver, drive, and drive fast."

He prodded the chauffeur with his gun, crouched low in the back of the limousine. The traffic cop was on the other side of the ambulance and Wentworth saw the interne stumble directly into his path, tangle with him and go down. The Lincoln, under the impetus of the gun, spurted forward. The cop couldn't shoot now with traffic so thick…. The Lincoln whipped into the park, the motor got deep-throated with speed. Wentworth lounged back with the revolver on his knee.

At his directions, the chauffeur turned out of the park into Fifth Avenue and headed back downtown. Wentworth warned him that any attempt to attract attention would mean a bullet through the head, and the chauffeur drove very circumspectly at Wentworth's directions. Kirkpatrick continued unconscious and worry began to gnaw at Wentworth's mind. He made shift to bandage the thigh wound, which was not dangerous, but the head wound must be more severe than he had thought at first. He must get Kirkpatrick to bed…. Rapidly, he went through his friend's pockets, found some letters to Corcoran Stanley at a West Thirty-Fifth Street address.

Wentworth had the chauffeur stop on a side street where there was little traffic and changed coats and hats with him. Wentworth did not scowl or threaten the frightened man, merely looked at him with his cold blue-gray eyes and smiled slightly.

"I am Corporal Death," he said pleasantly. "I would appreciate it if you didn't report the theft of the car for fifteen minutes. You may go."

THE MAN backed away, his eyes wide and frightened, and hurried off down the street. Wentworth sprang behind the wheel and drove away. The address was an old, remodeled building, and the apartment of Corcoran Stanley, the mail boxes showed, was 2-D. Wentworth tried keys on Kirkpatrick's ring until he found the right one. The apartment was small, a living-room and a kitchenette, a davenport that became a double bed. When his friend was stretched out there, Wentworth hurriedly drove the car a half-dozen blocks away and abandoned it. Then he returned to the apartment.

He was about to unlock the door, when he thought to listen first. He pressed an ear to the panel, could hear footsteps moving awkwardly about within the apartment. Kirkpatrick had recovered consciousness. It was a good sign. If the injury had been a fracture, he would not have roused. The limping footsteps retreated, a door slammed and Wentworth slid inside, saw that Kirkpatrick was in the bathroom, where water splashed vigorously. Clothing was laid neatly upon a chair. Wentworth nodded and went into the kitchenette, leaned against the wall to wait. He did not care to involve Kirkpatrick in what well might be a losing battle.

No one of Hoey's men now living had seen Kirkpatrick's face, whereas Wentworth had been spotted by several. Ultimately, police would link the chauffeur's report of a car stolen by Corporal Death with that other fiasco at the Mayfair Hotel. The attempt would be laid at his door. His shoulders were broad enough to carry it, but Kirkpatrick was not made for such furtive business....

The door of the bathroom opened and he saw Kirkpatrick limp to a spot where he could brace a hip against the table while he burnished his hard body with a coarse towel. Time after time, his eyes strayed to the bandage upon his thigh, made with two handkerchiefs. He finished with the towel, re-bandaged his leg, began painfully to dress; took a long pull from a bottle of brandy. When he had clothed himself, he dropped into an upholstered chair and sat disconsolately, his legs thrust straight out before him, his head hanging. The gray at Kirkpatrick's temples seemed almost white tonight and the harsh lines of determination about his mouth were lax and weakened. His was a strong, saturnine face, and it had been turned toward many a hopeless battle with courage. Kirkpatrick raised a hand and pressed his face hard against the palm, stayed that way for a long time.

Wentworth straightened away from the wall, took a half-step forward. His friend's despair was obvious. He had played his strongest card tonight, and he had seen his supporters fall in death, had met failure. At the hands of the men who had deprived him of honor and office, he had suffered this gravest defeat. Why shouldn't he comfort his friend? Wentworth asked himself. Why not reveal his presence, take his friend into the battle with him? He lifted a hand, opened his lips… then shook his head. No, there was another, better way for Kirkpatrick, and it did not lie along the perilous path of Corporal Death….

FINALLY, KIRKPATRICK got painfully to his feet and limped to a desk set against the wall, picked up a pen. He began to write what were obviously difficult words, for his face was rock-hard, the chin jutted. Still there was despair there and it came to Wentworth overwhelmingly that what Kirkpatrick wrote was his final message. For, peering around the corner of the door, Wentworth saw that Kirkpatrick had laid his revolver on the desk beside him and, now and again as he wrote, he glanced toward the gleam of the gun. Always there was a painful tightening of his eyes. He sighed heavily, and went on. Wentworth smiled sorrowfully. He had himself plumbed the depths of despair, but always the cause of service had driven him on. Sometimes death seemed pleasant by contrast…. He looked about the kitchen, saw a nickel-plated bell affixed to the wall. His eyes brightened. Quickly, he stepped upon a chair, used his knife to close the contact by crossing the wires. The bell rang sharply. Wentworth let himself softly to the floor. Gun in hand, Kirkpatrick was limping to the front door.

It was a dangerous thing Wentworth did then for his friend.

He crossed softly to the desk where Kirkpatrick had been writing, stood for a second staring at the hard, vertical script of Kirkpatrick. Even in this letter, there was no weakness. Swiftly, Wentworth drew from his vest pocket a platinum cigarette-lighter—the one thing he had saved from his previous existence. He thumbed off the base, pressed it against the letter, then stole back to the kitchen.

Kirkpatrick, at the door, whipped it open and stepped out into the hallway. There was no one there, nothing. He stared at the black staircase, at the neighboring doors of apartments, was seized by a sudden thought and whipped about to stare behind him. His room was empty, too. Slowly, he closed the door and walked with his painful limp back to the middle of the room. His memory of the bell was already hazed. Had it been as clear and sharp as it had seemed? Was it possible that it had been in the next apartment? He shrugged. It must have been.

He moved back toward the desk, dropped into the chair and his body stiffened. His hand on the revolver became a clenched fist. For there, where his pen had left the paper, there glowed a tiny figure limned in rich vermilion—a thing of hairy legs and poised, venomous fangs—a thing that had brought terror to the hearts of a thousand criminals, *the seal of the Spider!*

"Dick!" Kirkpatrick cried. "Dick!"

He lurched to his feet, staggered into the middle of the room, darted into the kitchen.

"Dick!" he shouted again. His voice was joyful, vigorous. QUICKLY, IGNORING the pain of his wound, he searched the apartment minutely and in the end he came back again to the letter that lay on his desk with the red seal that had written *finis* to his thoughts. There was no doubt in Kirkpatrick's mind. The man he had thought dead—who alone could resolve his doubts and end this poisonous misrule—was alive. Dick Wentworth, the Spider! His mind flashed back to that man who had strangely fought for him in Hoey's office and suddenly Kirkpatrick threw back his head and laughed.

Of course, fool that he was! Who else could it have been but Dick! Who else could have overcome those three police there in the hall at the end? Kirkpatrick laughed again. His shoulders were braced back again. He looked down at the letter, snatched it up and crushed it in his fist. Why, if Dick was alive, hope was not dead. He hurled the crushed letter across the room and stood with his legs braced apart, his chin lifted in that indomitable pose that Wentworth knew so well.

Outside the window, standing with a foot on the sill of the kitchen window and the other on that through which he peered to see his friend, Wentworth beheld that proud, fighting stance and a smile tugged at his mouth corners. His vision blurred suddenly and his lips moved in soundless curses. Damnable to have a man like Kirkpatrick put such faith in him. It made him feel strangely humble, curiously helpless and small….

Yet he knew that if Kirkpatrick, there in his poor little room, could have such faith—could come back from such depths of despair at the glimpse of that little red seal—then he had given him reason to hope.

Kirkpatrick's faith revived his belief in himself. But he would

"To the City Hall!" Wentworth cried.

"Demand Kirkpatrick for Commissioner!"

need Kirkpatrick's faith—aye, and his strength, too!—if he were to succeed in this greatest test of the Spider!

## CHAPTER 12
## NIGHT VISIT

WENTWORTH MADE his way cautiously down a drain-pipe and strode away into the night. It came to him overwhelmingly that he had accomplished very little thus far against the Mayor of Hell. Even now, he had no plan of campaign except to find the man and kill him. Somehow, that seemed strangely inadequate. It was true that the man's forces, his spokesmen, and criminals received the impetus for their vigor and intelligence from him, but there were other power-ful men in the organization, too. Killing the Mayor would be a telling blow—but it would not be final victory. The police force would continue corrupt and while they were indolent in their enforcement of the law, crime would wax and spread.

If only Stanley Kirkpatrick were again Commissioner of Police, he could do a very creditable house-cleaning within forty-eight hours. Well then, Corporal Death must see to it that New York City's puppet mayor removed Fogarty and put Kirkpatrick in his place! That would be a start toward victory.

Walking briskly along the frozen pavements, Wentworth threw back his head and laughed sharply. At the very outset, he seemed to encounter impossibilities. How could he make that man of no courage, Mayor Coddington, who had yielded to Senator Hoey and his undercover master, turn against the men who had made him? Yet Corporal Death must find a way... With a strong police force, it would be possible to begin elimination of the crooks in public offices, in itself a tremendous task. The prospects made Wentworth's shoulders sag, put weariness into his brain. He could not—yet he must... For the present he must rest.

THE NEXT day, Wentworth was early astir, upon the streets, before the morning rush to offices was over. He had set his task for the day. He must begin to create an overwhelming demand for the reinstatement of Kirkpatrick as Commissioner of Police. The people still had power, though it was doubtful if they realized it. Concerted action, an entire city aroused, could not be long defied even by the Mayor of Hell.

Wentworth was hampered immediately by lack of a medium through which to reach the people. With newspapers utterly subsidized, he had no resource.

There was one other thing he could do. It involved going on the prowl for some of the thousand crimes being committed daily in New York City. With the increasing frequency and boldness of such operations, he felt that to succeed he need only seek out places most likely for robbery and keep them under surveillance.

It was mid-afternoon before Wentworth came upon a suspicious scene. There was an automobile parked in the forbidden space at a bank entrance, its engine running and a very dignified-seeming chauffeur behind the wheel. Wentworth took a nonchalant stand against the bank wall and watched. The chauffeur's imposture was perfect, save for one thing. At too frequent intervals, he sent a glance sidling toward the doors of the bank.

Wentworth walked up the street, crossed and approached the chauffeur's side of the car, tucking his hat under his coat so that it would seem he had just come out-of-doors.

"Listen," Wentworth said sharply, "you can't park in front of the door like this. You'll have to move on."

"I'm just waiting for somebody, sir." The driver was very humble despite the shallow hardness of his eyes. "It won't be but a moment."

"You'll have to move on," Wentworth insisted. "Come on out now before I call a cop."

The chauffeur was very obviously stalling for time. Wentworth was almost sure that he was a driver for criminals. If the man would only make some overt move....

It happened, just as the thought flicked through Wentworth's brain. The door of the bank whipped open and three men in a close wedge spurted out, suitcases in their left hands, guns in their right. Even as they burst out into the street, the alarm bell at the corner of the bank building hurled a mad clangor into the street. The chauffeur's hand whipped to his coat pocket, dragged out a gun—but it was Wentworth who fired the opening gun of the engagement. He shot the chauffeur through the head and the impact of thirty-eight caliber lead hurled the man sideways to the cushions. The crash of the revolver halted the three bank bandits on the steps, guns questing for the source of the shot. THEY DIDN'T find it until Wentworth had fired twice more, and then it was too late for two of them. They crumpled on the steps of the bank in slow, surprised contortions, guns and money bags dropping first. The third man launched into a headlong charge for the auto, shooting as he came. He had located Wentworth, but it did him little good. Only Wentworth's eyes and forehead showed above the far side of the car and the bandit had to lift his gun very high even to stand a chance of scoring a hit....

The bandit fired twice and Wentworth discharged his third shot. The third robber went down on his face on the street. His gun flew from his hand and hit the side of the car with a tinny *thunk*. It was all over as quickly as that, yet Wentworth's marvelous marksmanship had killed four men!

Wentworth walked around the car, stooped over the third bandit and flopped him to his back. He whipped the long knife out of its sheath and marked the man with the Cross of Corporal Death. He went back to the auto then, stepped to the running board, the hood, then the top, looked slowly about him.

A dozen men and women were wedging out of the door of the bank, but they shrank back at sight of the dead. Windows in surrounding office buildings were slamming up and crowds that, a moment before, had been scattering to safety were cautiously coming back.

"The bandits are dead!" Wentworth shouted, lifting his hands. "I killed them. Come here and let me talk to you."

More people from inside the bank were pressing against the doors, a hundred others within sound of his voice crowded close to stare down at the dead men. They peered up at Wentworth curiously—until a man saw the cross of blood upon a dead man's face.

"Geez!" he whispered, "it's the Cross of Corporal Death! That—" His hand pointing, his voice rising to a scream—"That man is Corporal Death!"

Wentworth smiled at the excited man, whose arm still rigidly pointed at his face. "Yes," said Wentworth quietly, "I am Corporal Death." He lifted his voice so that all of them could hear. "One honest, uncorrupt policeman could have stopped this holdup. One man. I did it. I say again, any single policeman could have stopped the bandits. But there are none. The cops are in the pay of criminals. Bribed. Paid protection money. You pay the police protection money. Your taxes are that. They take your money and double-cross you in favor of crooks who rob you—as these men would have done.

"Listen, there is one way to stop this crime—to stop criminals from corrupting the police. Put a man in charge of the police whom you can trust, whom everyone can trust. We had such a man and you liked him so well you made him Governor of the State. He was put out of that office by the same plotters who are robbing you now. By crooks. Bring him back, make Stanley Kirkpatrick Commissioner of the Police and bribery and corruption will end."

There was a restless murmur through the crowd. Even as Wentworth had grimly forecast in his own mind, a man who has killed four fellow men speaks with authority.

Wentworth bent forward, pointing a rigid arm and forefinger. "*You* can bring back adequate police protection; *you* can cause the city to be run as you wish. *You* are the city, the bosses of the city. Why do you stand here idly while crooks run your city and rob you in a thousand ways? The very newspapers are afraid to speak! They have been bought by the criminals, or closed down by the militia of Senator Hoey. And you, the bosses of the city, permit it!" Wentworth's voice rang with scorn. "You are worse than the criminals who lie dead at your feet, worse than the policeman who takes a bribe. For you permit yourselves to be made fools, to be robbed. Why don't you take back your city from the crooks?"

"How, how?" The question came from one man, then another until it made a restless murmur through the ranks. In the distance, a siren made a faint wailing, minutes late. Much later than was necessary.

WENTWORTH JEERED. "The police are coming, when it's too late for them to help. You know what they will do? They will arrest *me*. Yet I am the man who prevented these robbers from escaping. *You* permit such things. *You* are to blame. Take back your city from the thieves."

*"How? How?"* This time the cry was angry, belligerent.

Wentworth leaned forward. "Go to City Hall. Demand to see the mayor and don't be turned away! Demand that he put an honest man at the head of the police force. Demand a man you *know* is honest: Stanley Kirkpatrick!"

The name struck a responsive chord in the ranks of people crowded close about the auto. They knew Stanley Kirkpatrick. Many of them had helped vote him into the governorship, for Kirkpatrick's election had been overwhelming. They would remember, too, that it was after Kirkpatrick apparently had been instrumental in putting down such criminals as now menaced them that he had been elected. Yes, they knew Kirkpatrick and respected him.

"To the City Hall!" Wentworth cried. "To the City Hall, and demand Kirkpatrick for Commissioner!"

Wentworth sprang down from the top of the auto and people backed away from him. This man had killed other men. He had put the Cross upon dead faces….

"To the City Hall!" Wentworth cried.

A murmur, then a shout echoed his cry. Wentworth moved off and the crowd swung into line behind him. A young man with his hair sprawling over a white forehead rushed up beside Wentworth. He lifted a clenched fist.

"To the City Hall!" he shouted. "We are the bosses of the city. We will boss it! Kirkpatrick for Commissioner!"

His voice brought a deep rumble from the ranks. They were only a dozen blocks from the City Hall and as they moved, the ranks thickened. The police radio car swerved to the curb just ahead of them and two cops ran toward the marching mob.

"Break this up," they snarled. "What's going on here? Come on, break it up!"

The youth who had sprung into the lead crouched before them.

"Crooks! Bribe-takers!" he snarled. "Go to the bank. A better man did your work for you. You are called to stop a bank robbery and you try to interfere with the people who pay your salaries. Crooks! Bribe takers!"

"Oh, a Red, eh?" said a cop. He reached out with his club and swung at the boy's head. It was the wrong move. The crowd closed in like water. The policeman grabbed for their revolvers, but they were overborne, hammered to the pavement where men and women kicked and pummeled them.

Wentworth waded through the ranks, knocking men aside. "To the City Hall!" he shouted. "The City Hall!"

HIS CRY caught and the two cops were left unconscious on the pavement while the mob surged on. It gathered strength as it moved. Men and women clung for an instant to its fringes and were infected by its mad virus. When City Hall Square was reached, there were a thousand in the thick-pressed ranks. They saw the heavy bronze doors of the building being swung shut and leaders broke into a headlong race to stop it. Police with guns in their hands sprang to the edge of the columned porch before the hall and fired over the heads of the crowds.

The mob's leaders slowed down, but the pack pressed them on, silent where before they had shouted. Right up to the steps of the City Hall the mob marched, surged like lapping waters toward the door. A policeman leveled his gun at the foremost ranks. From somewhere in the mob, a half brick sailed through the air. It caught the policeman in the face and hurled him down. A man sprang from the ranks and caught up his revolver, blasted at two other police who were near him. They went down, but the man who had shot them died, too. He fell waving the gun in the air, shouting: "Kill the crooks! Kill the bribe-takers!"

The other police went down before the assault of the crowd, yanked at the bronze doors. Wentworth stepped aside and let them race by. They could deal with the mayor and the rear ranks were the point of danger. Within minutes, emergency wagons from headquarters, armored motorcycles bearing machine guns would converge on the square. The mob could not stand against that.

Up along the hall, a door crashed open and a woman screamed.

"The Mayor!" chanted the mob. "We want the Mayor!" "Give us Kirkpatrick!" "Kirkpatrick for Commissioner of Police!"

They would have to retreat now, dispersed with a slashing of nightsticks. But they had got their message home to the Mayor.

Wentworth stepped out on the porch of the City Hall. The youth of the white face and straggling hair stood at the top of the steps, shouting, waving his arms. More hundreds had gathered to find out what it was all about and he told them, "grafters, bribe-takers, crooked police." He shouted Kirkpatrick's name… then the police came at a hard run. An armored motorcycle jumped the curbing and hammered across to the steps. The machine gun's muzzle was turned toward the mob. The boy at the head of the steps grinned at it.

"We are peaceful citizens," he yelled, "exercising our privilege of petition. We're going to put an honest man at your head again—Stanley Kirkpatrick."

The cop behind the machine gun was grim-faced. "It's a swell idea," he said, his brogue as wide as the Hudson. "But for what reason do you have to be killing honest cops?"

The boy spat eloquently, "We don't kill *honest* cops."

Wentworth tapped the boy on the shoulder. "Beat it, old

man," he said softly. "They'll give you ten years for daring to talk back. I'll take care of them."

The boy turned, defiance on his face until he recognized Wentworth. He braced himself and saluted with quivering vehemence. "Right, Corporal Death," he said, and hurried into the building. His voice had been thin, a little childish at the last, and it had carried as a falsetto will. Wentworth faced the police, marching cordons of them with guns in hand, a machine gun mounted on a motorcycle. The crowd melted away.

"Corporal Death!" called the machine gunner. "Corporal Death, come down here and surrender or I'll blow your blasted innards out through your back!"

## CHAPTER 13
## A DARING ATTACK

WENTWORTH LOOKED slowly over the scores of policemen who could bring their guns to bear on him, at the man behind the machine gun. There was a smile on the face of Corporal Death, but there was no mirth in his heart. Were all his well-laid plans, only just begun, to be smashed by the accident of a boy's high piping voice pronouncing his name? No, no, he could not fail now. There must be some other way, if he were quick.

Wentworth forced his smile to widen. "I'll surrender if Commissioner Fogarty orders it," he said quietly. "The Commissioner is inside the building now and, I'm afraid, he is in the power of my men." Wentworth turned his head toward the broad doors behind him.

"Commissioner Fogarty," he called, "is it your wish that I surrender?"

The harsh voice of Fogarty answered, somewhat muffled from behind the doors, it appeared.

"Who the hell wants you to surrender? I'm in charge here."

Wentworth was no ventriloquist, but he could imitate another man's voice to perfection and it was his eyes, looking at the heavy doors, which appeared to give direction to Fogarty's voice.

"That's a trick," the machine gunner shouted, though somewhat ill at ease. Four policemen were closing in on Wentworth, creeping up the steps from both sides with their guns in their hands.

"No trick," Wentworth told him. "Four of my men have got their guns on the Commissioner. Naturally, he understands that as long as I am held prisoner, he will be held, too. Bring the Commissioner out, boys!" Wentworth turned even more toward the broad doors. "Bring the Commissioner out!" he shouted.

He altered his voice, kept his lips motionless and made an unintelligible muffled response.

"What did you say?" he shouted. He took two long steps toward the door. "I don't care if he is fighting. Knock him over the head and bring him out!"

Behind him, the policemen had continued to close in. They were no more than ten feet behind him and, squeezing together inside the columns, they all but blocked off the machine gun. The gunner shouted furiously to them to get out of the way....

"Bring him out," Wentworth shouted angrily. "Bring the Commissioner out, or I'll…." He took two more long strides, caught hold of the door knob. There was a startled shout from the policemen just behind him. Their guns blasted, but they were too late by moments. Their lead clanged on the bronze doors. One bullet whisked through the narrowing opening and plucked at Wentworth's coat, then the door jarred sullenly shut. He was inside, safe for the moment.

Wentworth dived into the crowd that still jammed the hallway. A dozen faces were turned toward him, mouths open vacuously at the sound of guns.

"The cops!" Wentworth shouted. *"The cops!"*

HEAD DOWN, arms working before him, he charged through the crowd and in his wake panic arose. Men hoarsely echoed his cry. The bronze doors swayed open again and three policemen tried to jam through at once, wedged each other to a stand-still, then burst free and stood, heads shoved forward belligerently, guns at their hips, scowling at the mob. Their appearance completed the panic Wentworth had begun. A woman screamed and the whole press began to surge along the hall, away from the police. Wentworth stopped his headlong rush lest his faster pace attract attention. He moved with the crowd, one man among a hundred fugitives. No one, save possibly the machine gunner, would be able to identify him except by clothing and Wentworth had already changed the most conspicuous item of his wardrobe by snatching a hat from another man's head.

The police harried the mob from behind. More cops outside

the door slashed at them with nightsticks, tried to herd them into captivity, but there were too many. Wentworth felled a policeman with a blow to the stomach and sprinted to safety with a half-dozen others. Two minutes later, smothering his panting breathlessness, Wentworth was walking swiftly across town toward the Hudson River. A smile twitched now and again at his mouth corners. This was the first wholly successful battle he had fought against the Mayor of Hell. It was a flanking attack, of course, a blow where the evil genius would least expect it, but it was no less strong for all that. While the first struggle was still partly under way, Corporal Death was ready to strike his next blow....

He entered a restaurant a block from the office of the *News-Press* which had been the last and boldest newspaper to succumb to the power of Senator Hoey. It had fallen only when militia had taken over the shop. There were four newspaper men at the bar. Wentworth, who knew their type so well, could not mistake them, shrewd oldish eyes in careless faces, sharp tongues and brassy nerve. He took a place beside them.

"Listen," he said, "you're from the *News-Press?*"

The man nearest turned bland blue eyes on him, blinking behind glasses.

"Sure," he drawled, "what used to be the *News-Press.*"

"Well, look," Wentworth had adopted speech to fit his half-shoddy costume. "Look, there was a rumpus up at City Hall a few minutes ago, still going on. A mob came down and crashed the Mayor's office, yelling they wanted some guy named Kirkpatrick for Commissioner of Police. They gave the cops hell until reinforcements came down."

The man slouched a little more over the bar.

"So what?" he drawled. "Big scoop, eh? It's probably something we can't print." There was bitterness in his words.

"We're not running a newspaper any more," another of them groused. "We're running a hooey sheet. Or Hoey, if you want to spell it that way."

"Like to print it, would you?" Wentworth asked. "Sure! Like to blow the lid off this little old town. All of us would, but fat chance, brother. Fat chance."

Wentworth smiled thinly. There was no one else near them. He looked slowly, intently into each man's eyes in turn. He said, softly, "I'll fix it so you can."

"You!" They laughed. "Who are you?"

Wentworth said, "I am Corporal Death."

Four pairs of shrewd eyes were on him now, looking him over very carefully. Queer folk, newspaper men. Hard-headed, not too scrupulous in many things, improvident, hair-brained, all the things a successful business man is never supposed to be, but many of them carrying a strange idealism like a sword. It galled them to falsify news to suit certain vested interests—Senator Hoey in this case. Fools, of course. Any man with a scrap of idealism could be classed that way in modern business, but gay, brave fools they were. They stared at Wentworth now, not fearing him, but curious, and skeptical.

IN THE end he convinced them of his identity—in the upstairs room where he bought the drinks—and he learned, too, what he needed to know about the paper, learned that these men would back him to the end for the sake of printing the truth in their paper. Not that the act had any intrinsic value to them except the fulfillment of an ideal at which they would have jeered if accused of possessing it....

Hoey had one man in the office, a former newspaper man named Schwartz. He had two armed bodyguards, there were two policemen in the main entrance hall. That was all.... It was Wentworth's job to dispose of these five men. The reporters would do the rest and shout to the city the demand that Stanley Kirkpatrick head the police department again....

Wentworth walked with the four men the final block to the office. The entrance was a hallway that led to the elevators. The cops stood just inside, and paid little attention to people coming in. After all, guards had been stationed here for weeks and nothing had happened. Wentworth was on the right of the four news men who pushed in together. When he was beside the policeman, he struck with stiffened fingers at the man's throat, caught him completely by surprise. He had scarcely started to crumple to the floor when Wentworth sprang across the hall toward the other officer. The man caught the quick movement, jerked up his club....

Wentworth's left hand caught his wrist. The man's chin was pulled down and he couldn't reach the throat nerve, so he slammed his right to the jaw. It jarred the policeman back against the wall. His uniform cap tilted up and bumped to the floor and Wentworth struck again. It was the blow of head against wall that did the trick. The policeman crumpled and this time Wentworth could get to the throat.

Wentworth looked up, breathing deeply through his nostrils. An elevator boy and the starter were coming toward him uncertainly. The four newspaper men watched curiously and there was, at the moment, no one else in the hall. Wentworth palmed a gun and directed it toward the two elevator men.

"Just rest easy," he ordered quietly.

The two men skated to a stop on the smooth floor and Wentworth pulled a pair of handcuffs from the policeman's belt, tossed it to Mitchell.

"Handcuff them in an elevator and run it to a floor they aren't using much. Fix them so they can't reach the lever or the emergency bell."

The newspaper man took the policeman's gun, turned toward the two elevator men.

"Come on, Aloysius," he cried gaily, "We're going for an elevator ride."

"But Mr. Mitchell," he said, "I don't know. What is all this?"

"We're going to put out a newspaper that isn't a hooey sheet," Mitchell said, gesturing the gun. He closed the elevator doors behind the men and the indicator moved over a semi-circle of figures. Wentworth dragged the policemen to a door that led to the basement, handcuffed their wrists together after passing the chain through the banister. They would be out for twenty minutes or a half hour—that nerve blow was severe—and by that time the paper should be almost ready to hit the streets.

MITCHELL WAS back when Wentworth returned to the

hallway. "I'm beginning to like this," said the newspaper man. "Listen, let me smack one of those bodyguards will you? The fat one? I've been hating him a long time...." He reversed the revolver and held the barrel.

Wentworth smiled at him. "Not that way," he objected and held his own police thirty-eight in his palm, forefinger wrapped about the trigger guard. "Hit with the side of the barrel, near the chamber. It's more effective and the gun is ready for use. Besides, you're not so apt to shoot yourself."

Mitchell tried it. "You ought to know, Death, old boy. By Gee, I think we ought to call you General instead of Corporal."

They went up together in the elevator. Their manner was light, but there was no mistaking their tension. Wentworth was silent, his face set. Two men were out of the way, but there were two more to be faced. They would probably be criminals and not so easy to take as the police. They would shoot first and ask questions afterward. He could not call on any of these newspaper men for help there. They were unused to violence and would be more in the way than helpful. Still, he had a plan that might work. He had a description of the guards—both heavy, pasty-faced men with sneering eyes and a truculent manner—besides particulars as to hair color and eyes.... He separated from the four newspaper men without a glance in their direction and went to the boy who sat at an information desk and ran a comb through sleek black locks while he looked at himself in a small mirror.

"I want to see Editor Schwartz," Wentworth said, "and I won't be turned aside by any foolishness. I'm a citizen and I've been a subscriber of this paper for fifteen years. The way they're kow-towing to Senator Hoey is positively obscene. You tell Schwartz I'm going to see him, or I'll make trouble."

The boy nodded carelessly and handed him a slip of paper on which to write his name and business. Wentworth shoved it aside.

"To hell with that nonsense! You go in and tell this Editor Schwartz what I said."

The boy grinned. He had seen them come in like this before and he liked to see the bodyguards go into action.

"Certainly, sir. Have a seat, and I'll tell Mr. Schwartz just what you said."

He disappeared along the hall, slapping the wall with one hand in time to a tune he whistled between his teeth. The hallway was narrower than the waiting room and Wentworth stood just around the corner projection, took the mirror the boy had been using and placed it on the floor against the leg of a chair so it gave him a view of the corridor.

He hadn't long to wait, and he smiled as he caught a glimpse of the boy returning along the hall with a wide-shouldered man behind him. The boy was still whistling, slapping the wall with his hand. He couldn't whistle very well because he was grinning so. Wentworth slipped his gun into his hand, flat against his palm in the way he had showed Mitchell.

The boy was one pace ahead of the guard and on Wentworth's side of the hall. When he stepped clear of the projection, Wentworth pushed him violently toward the man. The boy's whistle broke in a gasp. He went against the legs of the guard and the man cursed. His hand shot to his coat pocket as he reeled backward. Wentworth stepped sharply forward reached out with his gun and struck.

THE BLOW caught the arm the guard threw up in defense. He danced back, got his gun free.... Wentworth's left hand whipped over his own shoulder and threw with the return. The knife pierced the man's right arm and the next time Wentworth struck with the gun, the guard went down. The boy was swaying groggily on his feet, trying to run and Wentworth caught him by the collar, hauled him back. It was a work of two minutes to bind and gag him with the unconscious guard. Wentworth put them in a closet that opened on the hall. Then he went rapidly toward the editorial room.

He saw a man peer out, then come rapidly toward him, recognized the hard, solid way he set down his heels, the slightly jerky sway of his shoulders. It was Mitchell. The newspaper man grinned when he came close to Wentworth.

"That wasn't the one I wanted to hit anyway. Say, suppose I take you over to Schwartz, then while the bodyguard is giving you the once over, I tap him behind the ear...."

"It's risky," Wentworth said, "for anybody who never tried it before. If you miss, you're apt to get shot."

Mitchell grinned, "I won't miss."

Wentworth shrugged. He would be glad of the help, God knew. He was tired, despite the stimulation of success, and there was still much ahead of him. Men said he killed in cold blood, but it was far from the truth. He was not callous. He would not flinch from his duty, but each lethal blow left its scar on his own soul.

"That editorial," Wentworth roused himself to say. "Ought to urge the people to go to city hall and urge Kirkpatrick as Police Commissioner."

"Inciting to riot, eh?" Mitchell said cheerfully. "Well, why not? You're inciting me to murder. It would be awful if I hit that guy too hard!"

Mitchell's manner became quiet and respectful as he led Wentworth across the wide editorial room. The editor's desk was in a corner, cut off from the rest of the room by rows of steel filing-cabinets. Near Wentworth was a long horse-shoe desk, with a man in the slot and others on the rim. They didn't look up as he went by with Mitchell. There were a score of other desks placed in rows and many were occupied. Typewriters hammered. A man called "Boy!" in an explosive, yet musical cadence.

AS HE neared Schwartz's corner, Wentworth saw that the editor was a small man with an irritable face. His movements were jerky and his voice, addressing a secretary, was harsh and domineering. As Mitchell and Wentworth showed at the entrance to the corner office, a heavy set man, muscles padded in fat, got up from a desk at their left and blocked their way.

"What do you want?" he growled.

"I want to introduce this gentleman to Mr. Schwartz," Mitchell said suavely. "He has a plan for making Senator Hoey President of the United States."

The guard turned his small, hard eyes on Wentworth. "Mr.

Schwartz is busy. Say, are you the mug sent in that phony message a while ago? Say, where's Bill…?"

He looked out over the editorial room and Wentworth moved forward a little so that the guard, in facing him, turned his back halfway toward Mitchell.

"Bill is indisposed at present," Wentworth told him lightly. "In fact, he's taking a nap out in the hall."

The guard said, "Wise guy, eh?" He reached out a big hand for Wentworth's shoulder. Wentworth shrank away and Mitchell struck with a looping overhand blow. Wentworth cursed. Foolish to have let Mitchell do a thing like that. He had moved his arm in too wide an arc. The guard couldn't fail to see the gun and…. What he had feared happened. The guard fell away, ducking under the blow and whirled with his gun coming out of his pocket. Mitchell was staring at him.

"Down!" Wentworth shouted. He was going for his own gun, but he saw that he would be too late. Unless Mitchell… Mitchell started down on his knees. The guard shot and Mitchell hit on his knees and bent far back on his heels, driven back by the man's bullet. As he went back, he lifted his gun arm stiffly and fired. Even a man who had never handled a gun before could not have missed at that pointblank range. But Mitchell did better than merely not miss. His bullet took the guard on the nose and smashed him back against Schwartz's desk. He hit the edge with the back of his head, bounced and sprawled down on his face.

Wentworth's gun was out as Mitchell fired and he lunged past the guard and reached Schwartz's desk even as the guard fell. He presented his gun just above the desk's top.

"Take your hand out of the drawer, Schwartz," he said softly, "and take it out... *empty!*"

"This is an outrage!" Schwartz shouted furiously. "Jenks, call the police, and tell them...."

He brought out his hand and it wasn't empty. He fired at Wentworth at point-blank range...!

## CHAPTER 14
## OUT OF VICTORY—DESPAIR

THERE WAS no time to dodge the shot, less chance that a bullet would be able to check the movement of the gun. Wentworth did two things with a rapidity that defied the ability of the eye to follow. His left hand, resting on the edge of the desk when Schwartz's shoulder hunched up with the speed of his draw, swept the telephone toward the gun muzzle. Wentworth's own weapon belched thunderously. Schwartz went backwards with the force of the bullet; his gun spat straight at Wentworth's body, but the interposed telephone caught the lead. The hard rubber was smashed to fragments, but the slug was turned aside.

Wentworth's left hand was numbed by the blow. He straightened slowly. Schwartz was dead with a bullet through the throat that had evidently severed his spine, for his head sagged brokenly on one shoulder. His body swayed gently back and forward in the swivel chair, a spring squeaking soft accompaniment. Then, as muscular rigidity left the body, it slumped, slowly at first, then gathering speed, slid under the desk.

There was no time to stand watching the antics of a corpse.

Wentworth spun about, leaped to the desk top. He had a gun in each hand and he sent his voice sharply over the editorial rooms.

"Stand still, everyone," he shouted. "There is no danger to anyone save the minions of Senator Hoey!"

The one newspaper man who had a gun drew his also and echoed Wentworth's command, while the other two hurried to Mitchell's side. Wentworth darted a single glance toward him, saw that his left arm was bloody and that he was already pushing up numbly from the floor where he lay. He grinned up at Wentworth.

"It was… worth it," he gasped, "to kill that louse. I did… kill him, didn't I?"

"You blew the back of his head off," Wentworth said succinctly. He dug out the gun he had taken from the guard in the hallway and handed it to one of the reporters. They went hurriedly toward the roomful of frightened men and women. Mitchell got to his feet, stubbornly maneuvered a chair until he could clamber on the desk beside Wentworth.

"Listen, gang," he yelled. "This lad is Corporal Death. He 'lows as how we ought to be allowed to get out the kind of paper we want—without dictation from Senator Hoey's little man Friday, by name Schwartz. It seems as how a mob went to City Hall today and said Stanley Kirkpatrick ought to clean up the police department and it's a wow of a story to print about Hoey. How about it, gang?"

A fat man without a coat, but with a vest swinging loosely from his shoulders and an eye shade shoved up off his forehead came striding across. He was over six feet and his belly shoved out belligerently ahead of him.

"Get down, Mitch," he said confidently, "What the hell's up now?"

Wentworth smiled at him gravely. "Mitchell covered the ground pretty well, Blake," he said, for he knew the man as he knew many of the newspaper officials of the city. "The *News-Press* prides itself on its independence and calls itself a crusading newspaper. I came here today to give it a chance to crusade against the damnedest combination of politics and crime the world has ever known. You know it, and...."

BLAKE LOOKED up at him and his mouth began to grin. "Sure, I know it. It gives me a pain. Tomorrow, we'll all be out on our ears if we're still alive, but meantime...." He turned around. "You mugs get busy. Carter, get Corporal Death's story. Martin, get downstairs and tell them there'll be a complete make-over on page one. Tell them to clean out page two and page three if they have to throw the type in the hellbox. Scrap the four o'clock edition. Get the circulation department and have Tom come up here...."

He turned around, his fat face almost impish, his eyes round and happy behind horn-rimmed spectacles. Wentworth put his guns slowly in his pockets, threw an arm about Mitchell just as he went faint with pain and eased him to the desk top.

"Game lad," Wentworth said, getting down to the floor.

Blake was standing with his thick legs spraddled out. "Tell Stevens to get over here quick," he bawled and a man with

143

bowed shoulders and a dead-white face came over at what looked like a leisurely pace.

"Here's the way page one looks now," he said.

Wentworth stepped up beside Blake and Stevens. "The object of the raid on the city hall," he said swiftly, "was a demand that Kirkpatrick be put in as Commissioner of Police. How about a two-column picture of Kirk and a five-column boxed editorial demanding that Kirk be put back in office? He's the only man living now who could step in there and do a clean-up job in a day's time."

Blake looked shrewdly at him. "Good idea, but we'll have to make the box four columns. Quicker setting. Want to write it?"

Wentworth grinned at him. "I expect to write it. By the way, will you tell Carter to stress the fact that the man who killed the police was shot down? I don't want any innocent persons to suffer for that."

Blake nodded: "You don't need to worry about this end any longer. The paper will go out and we'll keep hammering on it until the militia shuts us up." He reached in the top drawer and dragged out a heavy automatic. The man's face twisted. It no longer seemed fat, but lean and hard. "I've been wondering how long it would be before I killed Schwartz."

An office boy ran up and a man in shirtsleeves came over at his heels. "New stuff, Blake. Looks like we need it on page one. Hoey's got the legislators passing a new steal, to appoint a financial dictator of the state, to be named by the governor. Dictator to have complete powers, bond issues without consent of electorate. They can steal a billion dollars with that. You know who the dictator'll be. Hoey. Constitutional amendment to do it, or something of the sort. Vote on it December 31."

"Two columns, centered under the editorial. Kick something inside," Blake said shortly. "Tell Carter to work in an insert. Proof of what Hoey is trying to do to the state. That sort of thing."

The man nodded, loped away. Wentworth's face was very grim. "He'll have the militia at the polls, only his people can vote. There won't be any doubt of the outcome. We'll have to block that, Blake."

"Yeah," Blake's eyes were sardonic. "The legislators will jump through any hoop he holds out for them. The people won't have a chance. We'll be shut up by then—the paper will."

"Could you get one of the Newark papers to try it, drop them from airplanes over here? If it went across, and we won, you'd have your pick of newspaper jobs all over the country. Something to shoot at, Blake."

Blake said, "Yeah." He was looking down at the gun in his drawer. He smiled. "If I'm alive tomorrow, I'll try it."

WENTWORTH HELD out his hand. "I'm making you a promise, Blake," he said. "You won't regret this day. The gang that's ruining the state will be smashed."

"If we live."

"No 'ifs' about it," Wentworth shook his head, smiling very slightly, but not pleasantly. "I tell you the gang will be smashed! You'll hear from me."

Wentworth's lips, too often grim, were smiling as he went swiftly along the hall. Another victory. God grant he would be able to march through to the end. He would, if he lived.... For a moment, Wentworth's thoughts flew to Nita, lying wounded because she had stopped to gaze on the man she loved. How could he ever make up to her the undying devotion and loyalty she gave him? And there were Ram Singh and Jackson in prison and the two men who had briefly followed him, wounded and doomed to prison, hard-fisted old Pat O'Rourke and young Len Roberts. His burden of grief was heavy.... He could not think of such things. They robbed him of strength and vitality and there was so much more to do, so many men to fight. How confidently his voice had rung when he had reassured Blake that he would triumph! How empty his heart had been in that moment.

It was weary work that Wentworth did in the days that followed swiftly, speeding toward the day when Senator Hoey and the Mayor of Hell would take over the finances of the State by means of a crooked election. Wentworth twice robbed the homes of crooked politicians to finance his work. Day after day, he sent mobs howling to the City Hall to demand that Stanley Kirkpatrick be appointed Commissioner of Police. Wentworth sent money to Blake, who was pounding at Hoey from Jersey shores and dumping thousands of papers into New York. It was a thin cry they raised, one that was not heard by a third of the people of New York. Blake's papers were fought at every ferry and bridge tunnel by the police. Mounted patrols hunted down Wentworth's mobs and slashed through them with swinging nightsticks and rearing horses. Still the battle went on.

The Cross of Corporal Death appeared on a dozen criminals, detected red-handed in their robberies. A policeman had died like that, too, with the proof of crookedness upon his body. The police hid that when they gave the story to Hoey-ruled newspapers and the hue and cry that demanded the death of the Corporal. Death dinned from the thunderous columns. Wentworth heard that Hoey had personally offered twenty-five thousand dollars for proofs of his death….

**ON CHRISTMAS** day, Wentworth slipped through the back alleyways toward the house of Dr. Higgins. It was early, and on the icy streets, there was only desultory traffic. A servant was astir in Higgins' house, that was all, and Wentworth easily avoided her, made his way, silent-footed, up the back stairway. He found the room where Nita still lay. Two weeks now since she had been shot. She was out of danger, weakly recovering. Into her room, Wentworth crept, feeling the strong beating of his heart. Nita's white face—he winced to see her so pale—turned toward him. Her eyes opened incredulously, then her sweet mouth moved in a smile and she held out a pitifully wasted hand.

"Oh, Dick," she whispered. "Dick, darling…."

A tear welled out of her eye, slid its slow jewel face across her cheekbone. Wentworth stood there with his eyes drinking in the sight of her. Then suddenly he was on his knees beside the bed, his head buried against her shoulder. Something hard came up from his chest and thrust into his throat and he bit the sob back savagely. He felt Nita's hand light as a kiss upon his hair, her fingers…. Her voice was stronger, more like the old rich contralto he loved.

"I knew you'd come today, Dick, lover," she whispered. "I

147

knew you'd come, if you could. I've felt so alone here without you, so out of things because I couldn't help you."

Wentworth lifted his head and smiled at her, found her lips.... But soon he must steal out of the house again. It was a brief, pleasant oasis in a wasteland of destruction and death; death he created himself in order to build for finer things. All that he did, killing the minor leaders of crime and crooked politics whom he could reach—stirring the daily demand for Kirkpatrick—was build-up for a coup which he could not spring until election eve. He dared not, for it might fail in the end and the election would be won by Hoey. If he waited until election eve—the day before New Year's Eve, it would be—he could at least block Hoey for that one day.

AT LONG last, the day before election came and he went wearily toward Kirkpatrick's home. He had to move cautiously these days with eighteen thousand police on hourly look-out for him, with fabulous rewards that totaled over fifty thousand dollars sharpening every eye, planting every street with a hundred traps for his feet. He had not seen Kirkpatrick since that night when he had left a seal of the Spider upon his desk. He had not needed to. Kirkpatrick had seen the path that Wentworth would have him tread and he had set his feet upon it. Hounded by hostile police, heckled and bedeviled everywhere he went, he still fought on. He threw his personal fortune into the breach, hired halls and auditoriums and shouted denunciations of Hoey and his ilk. He had gathered a small group of wealthy and determined men about him and they had surrounded his efforts with armed guards who gave even Hoey's ruffians pause.

Yes, Kirkpatrick had maneuvered as well as Wentworth could wish and now the time had come to strike.

Wentworth entered openly the apartment house of Kirkpatrick and took the stairs to his second floor rooms. The only sound that reached his ears was the regular slap-slap of tire chains as a taxi drummed past on the street. Out of that soundlessness, Wentworth gathered a waiting tension that was painful in its intensity. His hand went to his revolver and his eyes stabbed into the half-gloom of the second floor.

He flung himself at the steps, went up with a swift, bounding stride, his gun in his hand now. The Mayor of Hell was too shrewd not to realize that all Wentworth's plans had been built around Kirkpatrick, around his becoming commissioner of police. Suppose he should…. At the door of the apartment, Wentworth hesitated even while his hand reached for the door knob. He pressed his ear against the panel, listening, listening….

There was no sound at all from within, not even such minor sounds as a lone man might make in his drawing-room. Wentworth had re-made some of the old devices of the Spider and he drew from a pocket belt about his waist a long, slender probe of surgical steel. It was a moment's work to turn the lock and, gun in hand, Wentworth lunged through the doorway. He went flat on his face and in the instant he hit the floor, an insane, thunderous burst of lead and flame burst over the house. Wentworth's revolver poked ahead of him, but there was no one to fire at—not a man in sight. Yet slugs from a sub-machine gun buzzed just above his head. Wentworth saw then what had been done, saw the machine gun braced with iron atop a desk, and the cord fastened to the door that had started the devastating fire… It was a gun trap which needed no human help to spring its murderous trigger.

Lying beneath that withering stream, Wentworth set his jaw rigidly. For this death trap could mean but one thing. Hoey's men had been before him, had done away with Kirkpatrick, and left this trap for his friend, the Spider! A numb agony settled upon Wentworth. With Kirkpatrick gone, all his plans were doomed to utter failure. At the eleventh hour, The Mayor of Hell had stolen his only chance of victory.…

## CHAPTER 15
## COUNSEL OF DESPAIR

WENTWORTH LAY there in an agony of mind greater than the pain those bullets might have inflicted upon his body, remained motionless until the sub-machine gun emptied its drum of cartridges. The silence that followed seemed enormous; then he heard a woman scream somewhere in the building. He got slowly to his feet, looked behind him at the wall. Bullets had eaten entirely through plaster and wood and smashed furniture beyond.

Wentworth laughed shortly. Fortunate that he had made a cautious entrance, or he would be lying, literally in two pieces, there on the floor. He hurried forward, saw that the gun had been screwed down to the table with prepared braces, that his entrance had tripped a heavy book-end tied to the trigger and that had held it back until the last bullet was discharged. He hurried through the apartment, seeking some clue to Kirkpatrick, but there was none. He felt a little sickened. There was a trembling in his stomach. He had escaped death many times, but that machine gun....

He hurried from the apartment building seconds before a police patrol skidded into the street, ducked into a restaurant bar for a drink. He stood staring into the mirror without seeing himself or the few others who, this early in the day, had entered the place. True, he had not intended to spring his coup until tonight, but with Kirkpatrick so obviously in the power of the Mayor of Hell, what chance had the Spider, who did not even know where the Mayor's hide-outs might be?

As he stared at himself, a cold hardness slowly spread over his face; his eyes lost their stare and became narrowed and speculative. It was a long chance that he glimpsed, but he must take it. He hoped that Kathleen O'Rourke was still at the Studebaker Hotel where he had registered her and given her money. He thought it likely she was, for she knew it would be dangerous to return to her empty home.

At the Studebaker, he did not inquire for Kathleen at the desk, but went straight to the room he had engaged for her, knocked softly. Nothing happened through long seconds, then the door opened cautiously a narrow crack, swung wide.

"I thought you'd never come back," Kathleen O'Rourke said breathlessly. "Come in."

Wentworth entered slowly, his eyes flicking once over the room that was empty except for themselves. He looked then into the deep blue of the girl's eyes. There were smudges of shadow beneath them, but she had not "let herself go." Her clothing was immaculate, and her dark-red hair lay in smooth, natural waves. She caught his hand in both of hers.

"Can't you help Pop and Len?" she pleaded. "I've been hoping and hoping. You… promised."

Wentworth studied her face keenly. Was she acting? Did she really hope that he would do something? He was sure that before now the girl, registered in her own name, would have been located by the Mayor's men. Her face told him nothing of all that. He covered her hands with his lean, strong one.

"That's why I came here today," he said. "I want you to make a deal with the Mayor of Hell, to surrender me for the release of your sweetheart and your father. He'll do it all right."

Kathleen's eyes widened on his face, "They'd kill you," she whispered. "They'd be sure to kill you!"

Wentworth smiled slightly. "The police are going to execute your father and sweetheart," he said. "And it's my fault that they're in trouble. I had a plan that would have freed them but it's no use."

"They wouldn't let me do it—Len and Pop wouldn't," Kathleen said "They'd say I was scum to do a thing like that. They didn't have to throw in with you. They wanted to. They hate Senator Hoey and the Mayor as much as you do. More, maybe. There was young Pat, you know, and…."

KATHLEEN'S VOICE choked off. She looked down at the floor, her hands clasped hard. Wentworth dropped down heavily on the bedside…. "You'll have to do it, Kathleen," he said shortly. "Orders. You swore to obey, you know."

152

Kathleen's head came up. There were little wet lines down across her cheeks and her eyes were glistening. She came to him and dropped down at his feet, put her hands on his knees.

"You're a fine, brave man," she said, "but I can't do it. It's just what the Mayor of Hell wants me to do. He found me here not long after you left and I pretended to do what he wanted. Otherwise, he'd have… done frightful things to me. But I can't do it, Corporal Death, Len and Pop wouldn't want me to. They'd…" She bowed her head against his knees and her shoulders shook. Wentworth stared at the blank wall of the room, his eyes narrow and hard. This wasn't trickery. He had intended to let Kathleen betray him, to trade places with Len and Pat O'Rourke not solely to free them, but to locate the Mayor's headquarters in a wild attempt to free Kirkpatrick….

Kathleen stopped crying presently, lifted her head. Her face was fresher, despite the redness.

"Now I feel better," she said lightly, sprang to her feet and crossed to a bureau to powder her nose. She talked over her shoulder while she used the puff. "I'll play the game my own way or I won't do it at all. I can't tell you how to reach them, but every day at about noon they call me up and ask me if you've come to see me. They're getting right impatient, but they're not suspicious. At least they haven't accused me of lying, yet…."

Wentworth's lips straightened and grew thin. So they weren't suspicious! That meant she was watched and they knew she told the truth to the extent at least of his not coming to see her. Fool that he was! He should have guessed she was watched. Had his despair blunted his intelligence?

He got sharply to his feet, locked the door. Kathleen turned toward him with widening eyes. "They're watching you," Wentworth explained shortly. "That's obvious from what you said. I don't want to be taken entirely by surprise. Now listen, I want you to go to George Blake over in Newark, the man who's getting out those newspapers against Hoey."

Kathleen nodded. She knew the newspapers, of course. The fact that police tried to keep the *Crusader,* as Blake had called it, out of the city, made it more sought after, more eagerly read.

"Tell him—" Wentworth's voice dropped, became more swift and sharp. If he was not mistaken he had heard a whisper out there in the hall "—Tell him that the Mayor of Hell has got Kirkpatrick and that I let them get me. Tell him I'll try to smash my way out with Kirkpatrick and take over the police department before midnight. If I don't—if I don't call him at that time, he's to publish these facts and demand government intervention. So far, there hasn't been anything to make the government step in, but kidnaping does it...."

As Wentworth talked, he had slipped the steel lock-pick from the belt about his waist and was working on the door that connected with the adjoining room. "He'll know that if I don't call him at midnight, it will be because I can't."

Kathleen stepped very close as he unlocked the door, looked up into his face with intent eyes.

"It will be because you're dead," she whispered. Wentworth laughed soundlessly, he bent and kissed her mouth as he would a child's. Her lips trembled, clung to his for a moment.

"Oh, you're *nice,*" she whispered. "I'll tell them. I'll...."

THERE WAS a sharp knock on the outer door and Wentworth pushed her through the opening, heard it bolted from the other side.

"Open up," a voice said harshly. "We know you've got a man in there."

Wentworth's lips twisted. So that was the stall that would be used! He moved toward the door. He could let these men capture him, or he could shoot it out and try to follow whichever one he allowed to escape. The former would be the surer, if they did not kill him on sight.

Wentworth slid a chair soundlessly to the door, stood on it to reach the transom. The voice outside was angry now. "I'll give you five seconds," it said. "Then we smash down the door. You can't get away, you know."

Wentworth peered cautiously out of the transom and knew he would not possibly be captured alive. It was assassination. One of the six men out there held a sawed-off shotgun and one had a Thompson gun against his hip. The others, with revolvers, were bunched behind them.

"Get out de way," the machine gunner growled. "I'll chew that lock out in two shakes, and saw him in two!"

Wentworth was glad that he had put his chair beside the door instead of in front of it. The house detective, who had been knocking, stepped back, muttered: "Okay. I warned them. Go ahead…."

The machine gun blasted and lead bored the door, cutting out the lock. Wentworth reached his knife across his shoulder and got it in his left hand. He leveled his revolver and shot the machine gunner through the head. The shot was drowned in the chatter of the heavier weapon and the men in the hall had no chance to act before Wentworth fired again. His second bullet dropped the shotgun man to the floor. There was silence for a choked instant in the hall, silence while machine gun and shotgun racketed to the floor. Then there was an overwhelming blast as the shotgun, cocked when it fell, discharged and blew the legs off the house detective. There were three other men and they hesitated there for an instant in the midst of the shambles, before they turned and fled.

Wentworth whipped open the door and raced after them. The detective shrieked wordlessly as he died. Ahead, the three men who fled were pretty well bunched, but one had almost reached the stair. Wentworth put a bullet through his back and the man spilled across the path of the other two, sprawled them hard to the floor. They rolled, shooting. Lead sang past Wentworth's ear. One of the men got to his feet and Wentworth put a bullet through his right arm. There was no chance for merciful shooting on the second man. He had rolled to the protection of his dead comrade and, resting his gun across the man's shoulder, fired carefully at Wentworth. The Spider's hat jerked up off his forehead and his gun spat a deliberate answer. The gunman's head snapped back; then flopped forward, and his feet drummed the floor convulsively.

Wentworth pocketed his gun, raced on. The wounded man had disappeared down the steps, but he could not have gone far. On the Spider's successful trailing of that man depended the entire outcome of his weeks of battling against the Mayor of Hell—depended the life of his friend, Kirkpatrick, the state and its people....

Frantically, Wentworth flung himself down the stairs, taking the steps in great, leaping strides while he balanced himself with a hand skimming the railing. Two floors below, on the fourth, he paused, listening. There wasn't a sound of flight. The hotel was in an uproar, but that was all. Determination brought a frown to Wentworth's forehead. Had he lost the trail upon which so much depended. God, he could not! He spun down the stairs, racing, racing....

## CHAPTER 16
## DANGER TRAIL

ON THE second floor up, he stopped again, listening. No wounded man could have run down the steps as swiftly as Wentworth had, and the gunman had had only a few seconds start. Somewhere the man had eluded him. Wentworth whirled toward the steps he had just descended and saw Kathleen round the platform above at full speed. She grasped the railing with both hands to halt her progress.

"On the fourth floor," she gasped. "Quick! I saw that man start out of a door, then duck back...!"

Wentworth took three steps at a time. Kathleen was already going upward with a swift beating of her high-heeled shoes, and he overtook her at the third floor, caught a hand under her elbow.

"As soon as the shooting stopped," Kathleen panted, "I ducked out into the hall and started downstairs..." Her eyes were wide with horror at the things she had seen… "On the fourth floor, I saw this man with the wounded arm…" They were on the fourth floor and she pointed toward a door. "He was in there."

Wentworth looked down at the floor, at the bloodstains the man had left. There hadn't been time to look before. The drops led to one room, back out of that to another. They didn't leave there and the door, to Wentworth's cautious hand, was locked. With a lithe spring, Wentworth caught the transom sill, drew his body upward until he could peer into the room. No one was in sight but he could hear a man panting with little moaning sounds. He muscled still higher and saw the man's shoulder. He was just beside the door with a gun in his left hand.

Wentworth lowered himself soundlessly to the floor again and led the way to the stairs that went upward. Out of sight there, he waited with Kathleen. He did not want to kill the man and there would be no other way of entering that room alive. He had not lost the trail yet. Doors opened along the hall and frightened faces peered out, men and women began to steal toward the elevator and stairs. It was apparent the gunmen had intimidated them, halted their earlier panic.

"Go, Kathleen," Wentworth whispered. "Something tells me our luck has changed now. You slip out of here with all these other people, and phone Blake as I told you. Leave word where I can find you at need."

Kathleen got slowly to her feet, a hand on his shoulder. "All right," she said. "Be careful, Corporal Death."

Wentworth watched her slim, rounded figure disappear at the corner. He smiled. The girl was made of good stuff. If he lived, he would fulfill his promise to her, free Len Roberts and Pat O'Rourke.

Wentworth pulled abruptly to his feet. A man was walking along with the crowd and he wore his overcoat like a cape. It was a smart idea, to hide that wounded arm with his overcoat, but he hadn't been able to do anything about the dark stain on the sleeve except to fold the sleeve on itself. It wasn't enough…

Wentworth went softly down the steps, got into the same elevator with the man. The chap's face was white and drawn with pain. He kept his feet braced wide apart as he walked across the lobby. Wentworth had no choice in what he did. When the man entered a taxi-cab, Wentworth got in with him, put his gun against the man's side and the cab got under way. He looked coldly, directly into the gunman's eyes. The man slumped back in his corner, head lolling on the cushions.

THE TAXI driver had noticed nothing out of the way and the car was droning along over the icy streets, slowing when it jounced over the deep groove of the car-tracks. Wentworth's lips were set in a slight smile. He got out his knife, turned its point toward the gunman. He felt no mercy, no pity. This man had been one of a gang intent upon murdering him, probably the girl, too. Wentworth slid the point through the man's trousers and let it prick his thigh. The fellow's head jerked up, his eyes wide in sudden terror.

"There's an artery just under this point," Wentworth explained softly. "If I shove the knife in not quite an inch, you will bleed to death before you can even get out of the cab." He put pressure on the knife and a gasp gushed from the man's lips.

"For God's sake," he whimpered.

"Sure," Wentworth jibed, "call on Him. Nobody else can save you…."

IN THE end, the man told that Kirkpatrick was taken to Queens—probably to one of two hideouts of which he gave the addresses. Afterward, Wentworth took the man to his hotel room where he bound him immovably to the bed after dressing the wound in his arm.

"If what you told me is true," he said shortly, "I'll come back and let you go. If it isn't…."

Wentworth went swiftly from the hotel, rented a drive-it-yourself coupé, sent it at a dangerous pace over the slippery length of Queensborough Bridge toward the second address the man had given. He chose that one because he believed the gunman would instinctively give last the one he thought most likely would be used. When he saw the place Wentworth felt a sharp certainty that he had guessed right.

It was a gaunt, low warehouse without windows except at one point on the front where there was an office.

Wentworth pulled the coupé sharply to the curb in front of the warehouse, went directly into the office. There was a girl and a man clerk there. The man got to his feet, moved furtively toward a filing cabinet and the Spider's gun snapped to his hand.

"Come here," he ordered softly.

The girl choked back a scream. "Oh, I knew something like this would happen," she whimpered. "I knew it. The boss ought not to let those men…."

The man clerk hit her across the mouth with the back of his

THE MAYOR OF HELL

hand. Wentworth vaulted the railing and caught him by the coat front. He shook him until the man's head wobbled.

"You have no manners," he said gently. "That's not the way to treat a lady." He shook him again, smiled toward the girl. "Go right on talking."

SHE HELD her mouth, shrank back into her chair and behind her the filing cabinet... *moved!* Wentworth drew back his gun again and when a man's head showed above the cabinet, he hurled the weapon violently forward. There had been no time to exchange gun for knife and there must be no noise to give the alarm.... The gun slammed against the man's mouth, crushed back his cry and Wentworth, driving the clerk violently to the floor with a single punch, reached the other man in two long strides. Wentworth's knife was ready now and, as the man reeled back, a hand to his shattered mouth, the other dragging out a gun... It never fired.

Wentworth had to let the man slump to the floor and spring back to the clerk. He was barely in time to step on his gun wrist and strike with the hilt of his bloodied knife. Wentworth turned toward the girl. She had fainted.... He sprang to the door the filing cabinet had revealed and stared off across the shadowed expanse of the warehouse. Light filtered in through the office and a few electric lights burned vaguely. That was all. An immense silence filled the entire place. If his arrival had been spotted, the criminals were waiting in silence to kill when he should show himself.

Wentworth returned to the office and tied up the clerk and

the girl, cut the telephone wires, locked the outer door. Then he returned once more to the filing cabinet.

Soft-footed, gun and knife in hand, Wentworth stole across the floor of the warehouse. There were piles of crates and barrels with narrow aisles between, plenty of cover for an army of criminals to ambush him. He crept on, toward those dim lights and the upright shadows that marked the elevator shaft.

In the thick shadows beside the shaft, Wentworth hesitated. The cage was at the first floor and its bottom was a little above the level of the warehouse floor. It might not mean anything at all, but the momentum of an elevator usually tended to carry it past, rather than short of, the level at which it was intended to stop. The elevator seemed to have come up from the basement, yet no light showed from below. Wentworth stepped onto the elevator. He reached the lever and, lips set in a straight, sardonic line, sent the cage downward....

The whir of the machinery seemed to fill the whole vast vault of the warehouse. Wentworth squatted to get an earlier view of the basement, but only darkness met his eyes. Abruptly then, when the elevator was half-way to the basement, there was a clatter below him and he peered over the edge to see that the bottom of the elevator shaft had opened up in a two-part trap door, revealing a sub-basement below.

Wentworth ducked back from sight, put a hip against the lever and palmed knife and gun again. His lips were curved happily. The gunman had not lied. The man he had knifed must have come up on the elevator or from this hidden basement and left whatever switch operated the secret doors thrown open for his return. The gods of luck were favoring the Spider at last. If only Kirkpatrick was hidden here....

"Geez!" a man cried below. "That ain't Hunky. Look at his feet! Shoot him! Shoot...!"

## CHAPTER 17
## KNIFE AND GUN

A CURSE sprang to Wentworth's lips. He had hoped to enter the quarters of the gangsters and locate Kirkpatrick before he was discovered, but the alarm was given irrevocably now. From the guard's cry, it was apparent there was more than one man there. One man might be settled silently with a thrown knife, but two of them....

Wentworth hurled himself flat on the floor, peering through the widening crack which revealed the sub-basement. There were two men and one of them was racing for a door across a small room while the other crouched with a gun ready in his fist. Wentworth dropped the running man, with a bullet through the back of his skull.

The second man fired almost simultaneously, and a splinter of wood from the elevator floor gouged across Wentworth's temple. The fellow turned to flee also and Wentworth whipped the knife in a hard overhand drive. It flew unerringly, pierced to the hilt beneath the left shoulder blade and the man went down hard on his face, arms spread-eagled in the instantaneous convulsion of death.

WENTWORTH SPRANG from the still-descending

elevator and caught his knife from the man's back on the run, dived through the doorway those other two had sought in vain. A burst of gunfire greeted him, but he had gone through the entrance fast and the bullets went behind and over him. He hit on a shoulder, rolling, stopped dead on his stomach and was firing in the same instant. The three men crouched behind a davenport were barricaded against the door, but Wentworth's quick leap had put him in a flanking position. It exposed them to his fire and put them in one another's way—for they stood in a line, side by side and Wentworth was at the left end.

Wentworth's first shot took the man on his end in the forehead as he whirled to fire, tipped him backward against his companions. The Spider's second shot missed a moving shoulder, and sticking his stained knife upright in the floor before his face, he groped in his pocket for the second revolver. He faced two armed men at a range of less than twenty feet.

The first gunman slumped to the floor and the second flung excited lead at Wentworth. The third was still tangled. The bullet hammered dust from the carpet within two inches of Wentworth's right hand. A second shot hit the blade of the knife and hurled it, hilt-first, at Wentworth's forehead. Wentworth got his two guns before him and, both living men in view now, he fired his revolvers the instant the hilt crashed against his forehead. Blinding white light smashed into his eyes, dazzled his brain. Wentworth tried to push himself up from the floor, but arms and legs refused his orders. He tried to squeeze the triggers of his guns again, but that, too, was futile.

He could not have been like that for more than three seconds, yet years of struggle seemed to fly past in the interval. Finally his hand obeyed his orders and dragged across his forehead, cleared his eyes of blood. He saw that all three gunmen were down, but that one of them was crawling toward the gun which evidently had been hammered from his grasp when he was shot. He got the revolver just as Wentworth's dazzled eyes focused upon him. Wentworth tried to lift his own weapon, but it seemed incredibly heavy. It was impossible to raise it, and yet he did. He tilted the muzzle up from the floor and fired. The gunman slumped down on his face, rolled on his side. His knees, slowly, agonizingly, drew up against his belly....

WENTWORTH STAGGERED to his feet, dragged out a handkerchief to dab at his forehead while his eyes stabbed searchingly about the room. There were three doors, all closed, and no one moved within his sight. He stooped slowly, painfully, recovered his knife. The bullet had struck on the blade, just short of the hilt, had bent the guard but not damaged it in any other way. Standing with his legs braced wide apart, Wentworth thrust out empty shells from his guns and put in fresh cartridges, wiped his knife clean and held it in his hand, point foremost, as he moved toward the three doors.

His head ached splittingly, almost blinded him at every movement, but he could not delay now. If Kirkpatrick were not here, he must go to the second hideout and kill, kill, kill, until he had freed his friend. He eased open the first door and found only a vast warehouse floor, stacked with boxes and bales and barrels. Wentworth guessed shrewdly that this was loot of some of the robber gangs under the Mayor of Hell. He moved to a second door.

It was an office, elaborately fitted out with lavish furnishings. Wentworth felt despair stab at him. Two of the doors had been futile. If the third did not reveal Kirkpatrick... Wentworth felt overwhelmingly tired. Pain ran in fiery serpents through his brain. He leaned against the wall, gathering strength, then moved heavily toward the third door. He turned its knob cautiously, pressed against it. Locked... He fumbled out the lockpick. His fingers seemed wooden. It took an interminable time to maneuver the bolt. He pushed open the door and a cry surged to his throat. He staggered into the room. Kirkpatrick was there, but he lay motionless upon a bed. There was a bloody gash across his forehead.

Wentworth bent anxiously over the bed, his hand flying to Kirkpatrick's throat pulse. Then happiness gushed like warm blood to his heart. Alive! And the pulse was strong and full! He could see now that the bloody streak was no more than a crease. Evidently one of those last three men he had slain had fired at Kirkpatrick when he heard the first shot, but Wentworth's attack had been too precipitate to allow him to complete his assassin's job.

Wentworth hurried about the room, found water and bathed the wound, massaged the back of Kirkpatrick's neck until, after ten minutes of strenuous effort, Kirkpatrick opened his eyes weakly. A smile stirred the hard line of his lips. "Good boy, Dick," he whispered, and closed his eyes again.

It was ten minutes more before Kirkpatrick pushed to his feet.

He faced Wentworth. "You look like you need some doctoring yourself, Dick," he smiled.

Not until then did Wentworth look into a mirror to discover that the knife hilt had lacerated his forehead severely, Dried blood spread like a bandage across his brows. He cleaned it off hurriedly, led Kirkpatrick toward the door. His friend stopped there for a moment, staring at the dead, stopped again in the outer room.

"Five men!" he said. "Good lord, Dick, how in the name of heaven do you go through these battles and come out unscathed?"

"I don't," Wentworth said, with a gesture toward his forehead.

Kirkpatrick grimaced. "But these five are dead!"

WENTWORTH SHRUGGED, gestured toward the elevator, "Few men can shoot well in excitement," he said. "They don't practice sufficiently. Furthermore, they've never learned that a little bit of cover is better than none at all. If those three in the other room had thrown themselves flat on the floor when I outflanked them, I'd probably be dead in there beside one of them."

"I think it's just bull luck," Kirkpatrick said.

Wentworth stopped the elevator, helped Kirkpatrick off at the first floor and led the way slowly across the warehouse. He was as buoyant now as he had been weary a few moments ago. Another victory had been won. True, most of the battle lay ahead, but at least he had saved Kirkpatrick.

"It's not luck, Kirk," he said, "unless you want to call it luck that I have spent, probably, an actual full year of my life on the pistol range, practicing until I can shoot as easily and well as most men can use their eyes. If three men are shooting at me and my first shot kills one of them—there really isn't much 'if' about my first shot killing—it throws the others into such a panic that they shoot wildly. And it doesn't throw me into a panic. I just pull the trigger twice more and there are two more dead men. The only thing that could save them would be for one of their number to remain cool, and to get in a shot before I shot him... And I always shoot the cool ones first. Someday, there will be more cool ones than I have time to shoot and on that day... exit Richard Wentworth!"

On the bleak street, the gray light of day was fading and the shadows against the buildings were blue. No one was in sight and Wentworth drove Kirkpatrick carefully away. It was growing even colder.

"I don't believe it," Kirkpatrick said abruptly. "They'll never kill you. You're immortal, a god, or at least a demi-god of battle..." He turned toward Wentworth. "By the way, Dick, thanks for rescuing me." He was a bit awkward about it, his hand on Wentworth's shoulder was tentative, hesitant. He wasn't a demonstrative man.

Wentworth laughed. "I don't suppose you've ever done anything for me?"

Kirkpatrick was silent for a while, and in the silence they were each conscious of the warmth of the bond that held them together. Kirkpatrick said soberly:

"What's on for tonight, Dick, that you could promise that girl release?"

Wentworth glanced at Kirk's strong, aquiline profile, the hard set of the jaw. Good to hear the old familiar clipped speech, to know that Kirkpatrick was vigorously ready to help.

"I want you to go to that Green Tavern and have supper," Wentworth said, "though you needn't make yourself too conspicuous. At nine o'clock sharp, come to police headquarters on Centre Street and up to your old office. The Mayor of the City will be there and he will appoint you Commissioner of Police!"

KIRKPATRICK SUCKED in his breath, turned toward his friend. Wentworth was looking straight ahead with a small, eager smile on his lips. There were times when he seemed almost boyish. It was as if all the great, lethal strategy were a child's game and that he felt he was winning....

"How will you manage that, Dick?" Kirkpatrick asked quietly.

Wentworth threw him a laughing glance. "That's my job," he said. "What you've got to do is to make sure that the police'll enforce fair voting at the polls tomorrow. In other words, clean up the force overnight!"

"So soon as that?" Kirkpatrick shook his head. "I'll do my best."

They had crossed over the dark cold reaches of the East River and turned downtown. Wentworth pulled to the curb. "This is where we part, Kirk. I'll see you later. I've got to turn loose the crook that told me where you were."

Kirkpatrick thrust out his hand. "I wish you'd let me help you, Dick...."

"Your work will come later," Wentworth said. Their hands

met, gripped hard. They smiled, both men thin-lipped, their eyes direct and hard.

"At nine o'clock, Dick."

"Nine o'clock."

## CHAPTER 18
## NINE O'CLOCK

IT WAS ten minutes of nine o'clock when Mayor Codding-ton's limousine drew up at the entrance of police headquarters and the chubby figure of the mayor got out, followed by a man whose movements were at once lithe and dignified. They went through the main door together and through the hall without gazing into the room where the sergeant sat behind his desk. Nevertheless, as they set foot on the second floor, the Police Commissioner's door opened and the official himself strode out.

Commissioner Fogarty had gray hair and his face was set in somber, positive lines. He should have been a fine figure of a man, from his build and the shape of his jaw and head, but there was one thing sadly amiss. His eyes wavered from a direct glance and strayed off over the mayor's shoulder.

"Hello, Coddington," he said, "this is an unexpected pleasure."

Coddington was a chunky man, but he had a hollowed, austere face. He was not a bad man, merely weak. Now he had the support of the strong man beside him—Richard Wentworth.

"Unexpected, I have no doubt," Coddington said drily. He went past Commissioner Fogarty without a second glance, sat down at Fogarty's desk. The Commissioner stood before it, big shouldered and strong-backed, with somewhat the air of a culprit before a teacher's desk.

"What's up, Coddington?" he asked, a challenge in his voice. He paid no attention to Wentworth, who stood over by the door with a quiet smile on his somewhat grim lips. His gray-blue eyes were almost happy as they regarded the mayor.

"This is up," Coddington said in the bullying manner of a small man who must play a big part, "I want your resignation, effective at once, or I'll fire you out as grossly incompetent, crooked and the sponsor of a corrupt department."

His words were delivered swiftly, drily, but with a positive force which surprised Wentworth slightly. He had been prepared to use force on the mayor if necessary to attain his end, but arguments had prevailed. The constant mobs that had hammered at Coddington's doors, crying for Kirkpatrick for Commissioner had not been without their effect and when Wentworth had pointed out to the mayor the fame that would accrue to the official who could take positive action in this great crisis of his city, Coddington had weakened. The governorship, the presidency even, Wentworth had implied, might lie waiting for him if only he could gather himself together and take the single positive action of expelling one police commissioner and naming another—the right one!

Even as Coddington had previously been swayed by the potency of Senator Hoey and the Mayor of Hell, so he bent now to the new storm that was called the Voice of the People, as represented by this quiet, authoritative man who had entered his house so unobtrusively that even the guards did not know he was there. So he had come with Wentworth to police head-quarters and was declaring himself in the manner of which he was so fond.

Fogarty was utterly silent, entirely motionless for perhaps thirty seconds after Coddington had spoken, then he bellowed.

"This is an outrage," he shouted. "I won't resign. You can't kick me out without reason!"

"I've given you my reasons," Coddington replied shortly. "You are a crook. The department is corrupt. Your resignation at once, or I shall have you arrested and thrown into a cell."

FOGARTY SPLUTTERED. He leaned over the desk and shook his fists in the air. Coddington, chunky and very calm, smiled up into his face. There was nothing of the physical coward about Coddington. He was only afraid of decisions. Once made, he clung to them with the panic of a drowning man.

Fogarty shouted himself out and Coddington took it with a tight, dry smile on his lips. Finally, he waved a pudgy hand in Fogarty's face.

"Resign at once, Fogarty. I have other important business to attend to."

Fogarty made a sudden leap for the row of buttons at the end of his desk, but he was bulky and unused to quick movement. Before he could touch a button, Wentworth's hand closed on his wrist, spun him sharply about. The wrist continued in Wentworth's hand and he pushed it well up between Fogarty's shoulder-blades. He held it there for five seconds, then turned the

Commissioner loose with an added jerk on the arm that sent him stumbling half across the office.

"Do you want to write that resignation," Wentworth asked quietly, "or are you just going to be fired?"

"Who in the hell are you?"

Wentworth smiled slightly, "Mayor Coddington's new body-guard," he said.

"Oh, throw him out," Coddington cried wearily. "I'm tired of fooling with him."

Wentworth took a step forward, but Fogarty dropped his raised hands. "All right," he said, "I'll resign." He did as Coddington ordered then, and turned the paper over to the mayor without further quibble.

"Good," said the mayor, "now you will kindly be seated unobtrusively in the corner there until your successor arrives."

Fogarty took refuge in a sneer. "He won't come," he said.

"Who?" Coddington asked quietly.

"Your new commissioner, Kirkpatrick. He won't come. He was kidnapped this morning and we've been trying to find him all day. We didn't find him."

Wentworth smiled. "But I did!"

There was no other sound until, clear through the winter night, a bell began to toll.

THROUGH THE somber, slow vibration of the bell, Wentworth felt his muscles stiffening. Suppose, suppose crooked police had seen Kirkpatrick at the Green Tavern…! The bell stopped striking and there was a brief rap on the door. It opened and a policeman stuck his head in.

173

"Man named Kirkpatrick…."

"Show him in, show him in," snapped Coddington.

The door swung wide and Stanley Kirkpatrick made an entrance.

Mayor Coddington came to his feet. "Good!" he said. "I like men who are prompt. Mr. Kirkpatrick, will you accept the post of Police Commissioner?"

Kirkpatrick nodded gravely, unsmiling. "I will be happy to."

"Raise your right hand," snapped Coddington, and rattled off the oath of office, nodded his head alertly at the end. "Fine, take over at once, Mr. Kirkpatrick. Fogarty, out!"

Within moments, Kirkpatrick was at the desk. Wentworth smiled to hear his crisp voice on the telephone.

"This is Kirkpatrick, new commissioner of police," he said shortly into the transmitter. "Yes, Kirkpatrick—thank you, Bogan, I'm glad to be back. Get all borough deputies on one wire and all precinct captains at once. Couple me at the same time with the radio broadcast to all cars. Have the announcer call all cars and have them stand by when you have the captains and deputies on the wire. Thank you."

He pressed a button and a secretary appeared with a languid slowness, munching on an apple. When he saw Kirkpatrick behind the desk, he stiffened, tucking the apple behind him.

Kirkpatrick said shortly. "Get me a complete roster of the police department—all sections. Have it here in two minutes."

The man sputtered, "Yes, sir!" fairly ran from the room.

Kirkpatrick turned to Mayor Coddington. "As soon as the telephone calls are arranged, and the radio," he said, "I'm going to ask you to tell the officials briefly that Fogarty has resigned and that I am the new commissioner. Do you mind?"

CODDINGTON SMILED and for the first time there was some warmth in his expression. "Not at all. In fact, I think I am going to stay for a while and listen to you work. You have a sound of efficiency, Mr. Kirkpatrick, and it is a rare thing in my government."

The telephone whirred softly and Kirkpatrick caught up the instrument. "Good, Bogan," he said quietly, "that's fast work... I am speaking," he went on, "to all precinct and borough commanders of the police and all radio patrol cars. This is Stanley Kirkpatrick, new commissioner of police. The Mayor wishes to speak to you...."

Mayor Coddington took the phone eagerly, but his voice remained dry. "Because I have been dissatisfied and the people of our city have been dissatisfied with the recent conduct of the police department, I have requested Fogarty to resign. He has resigned and I have appointed in his place the man who in the past has been the best Police Commissioner and the best Governor this city and State have ever known. He has complete authority. No one will or can interfere with him. He has one order and one order only: Clean up the city."

Stanley Kirkpatrick took back the telephone with a smile and a nod. "Thank you Mr. Mayor," he said. "Men, I have only one message to you at this time. You will do well to heed it in its every syllable. It is this. There is no longer such a thing as special privilege in this city...."

Wentworth heard that much before, with a quiet smile on his

lips, he went hurriedly, unobserved, from police headquarters. There was more work for the Spider. Up in the square, bare office of the commissioner, Coddington's eyes were speculative upon the door by which he had left. When Kirkpatrick had done with his talk, he asked a question.

"Who is that man, Kirkpatrick?"

Kirkpatrick's face was very grave. "He is the finest man it has ever been my privilege to know and work beside," he said. "He is utterly unselfish, a strong and brilliant man. Richard Wentworth."

Coddington smiled his dry, tight-lipped smile. "Now, I have no more fears," he said. "Now I know we will win."

## CHAPTER 19
## WENTWORTH'S BIT

IF WENTWORTH could have heard Mayor Coddington pronounce his certainty of victory, a sardonic smile would have touched his lips. If only Coddington knew on what a slender hope their victory depended!

He had struck a telling blow in rescuing Kirkpatrick and compelling his appointment as police commissioner, but the real job, the ultimate responsibility rested on his own shoulders. He had made a single request of Kirkpatrick that he knew would be attended to at the first opportunity—the release of Ken Roberts and Patrick O'Rourke.

His first action, on leaving the vicinity of police headquarters was to find a telephone and call Blake. He told him in sharp sentences what had happened.

"If you've done that, the end's in sight," Blake chortled. "Man, Corporal Death, you're a ninety days' wonder. May it be ninety years!"

Wentworth felt a slight impatience surge through him. He broke in shortly on Blake's jubilation, demanded where he could get in touch with Kathleen O'Rourke, called her promptly.

"Kathleen," he said, "this is—"

He got no further than that. "Thank God you're safe," she said. "I followed you to Queens and saw you go into that warehouse, but while I was looking for a friend of Len's that was honest and would help, you came out and went away. Or at least your auto was gone...."

Wentworth let her gush it all out, then he told her that her sweetheart and father would be released in a short while from Bellevue Hospital where they were still guarded, that she was to meet them as they came out and bring them to the corner of Twenty-fourth Street and First Avenue in a taxi....

AT ELEVEN-TWENTY, a taxi drew up beside the limousine Wentworth had rented, under an assumed identity and a man on crutches and another who moved with the slow heaviness of a man still weak on his feet came toward the car. Wentworth felt his heart sink as he saw them. They could not help him. He had not thought they would be so weak... They climbed into the limousine and the taxi pulled away. Pat O'Rourke clasped Wentworth's hand in both of his.

177

"The Virgin bless you, sorr," he said huskily. "I knew you'd be after getting us out."

Len Roberts said, in worried tones, "I hope we'll be able to help, Corporal. I can still use a gun." Kathleen sat beside him and gazed proudly at Wentworth.

"Sure, you can help," he said gaily. He started the limousine carefully forward. The tires skidded a little, then caught hold and sent the car lunging out into First Avenue and northward.

"What are we after doin' this night?" Pat asked anxiously, still leaning forward.

WENTWORTH SAID soberly, "I'm going to kidnap Senator Hoey and take his place."

He drove a full block in utter silence, then Pat laughed with something of his deep old heartiness.

"Mary bless my soul!" he gasped. "If you don't take the cake!"

Len Roberts said quietly, "What's the plan, Corporal?"

Wentworth's heart sang. These men were crippled, but they did not try to discourage him, only sought to help. If he could not win with their help, he would never win at all.

"I'll go to Hoey's bedroom," he said briefly, "gag and bind him and lower him to you. You take him in the car and keep him there, that's all. If I leave the house, you are to follow me. After that, use your own judgment."

"Do we keep Hoey alive?"

"Yes, we may need a hostage."

A block from the private house on East Sixty-ninth which Senator Hoey occupied, Wentworth turned over the wheel of the car to Kathleen.

"In fifteen minutes, drive along Sixty-ninth. I'll be ready then if ever," he instructed her.

There were two patrolmen in front of Hoey's home. They stood together in the doorway, sheltered from the sharp wind that whimpered up the streets. They stopped talking, stepped forward alertly when he swung briskly up the steps to Hoey's mansion.

"Hold on," one challenged, "What do you want?"

"The Senator," Wentworth replied glibly to their question. He kept on up the steps, abruptly sprang toward the two police. He went past the left hand side of the first one, and swung at the back of the man's head with his clubbed revolver, felt it strike and dived head-first into the belly of the second. It was all one continuous movement and the first policeman had not hit the pavement when Wentworth bore the second man back on the steps. It was a work of seconds to slug him also with the gun.

He went up the steps to the front door. From the belt about his waist, he drew a keen glass-cutter, ran its rasping edge along the glass panel of a door. A suction disk, applied to its center, pulled it toward him. He stepped alertly through, merged into the shadows of a corner to the right of the portal. The sound of the glass cutter must have reached through the house, and there were inside guards… Yes, he was right. A man came furtively down the front steps in the hall, a gleam of metal in each hand, hand-torch and gun. Wentworth snaked his knife out of his between-shoulders sheath, let it lie flat on his palm at his side. He tried not to think that a single slip meant ruin….

THE TORCH blazed light almost directly in his face and

Wentworth's knife hand jerked forward. He went in behind the flicker of steel, caught the man's two hands an instant after the steel found its sheath in his throat. He stood on the man's feet. Convulsive quivers shook the body, then there was an inert sagging. Wentworth eased the dead man to the floor, drew out his knife. He went swiftly then to the front door and lifted the glass panel back into place. Three minute strips of glue-paper fastened it back in place. He left the man's body upon the floor and went soundlessly up the stairs. Three guards disposed of without an alarm. Wentworth's heart began to beat high with hope.

Half-way up the flight of stairs, he paused, searching the dimness of the hallway above. He saw a man seated in a chair, its back tipped against the wall. The guard turned his head....

"Frank?" he called cautiously.

Wentworth had no way of telling in what voice the man he had slain would talk. He chanced a mumble....

"Damned cops," he grunted.

The guard settled back in his chair, then stiffened, staring at the dark figure approaching him. Wentworth caught the first movement and hurled himself forward in long, bounding strides. The man slapped his chair legs down, tried to get to his feet. His mouth opened for a cry. Wentworth threw the knife, saw it pierce beneath the chin and drive upward, push the man's head back with the impact of the throw. The chair crashed to the floor.

Wentworth made no effort then to ease to the floor the body of the man he had killed. He whipped his knife free, yanked open the door the man had guarded and sprang toward the bed he saw vaguely. A heavy figure reared up awkwardly on an elbow in the bed and Wentworth struck savagely with his fist. The man slumped down again and Wentworth bent close. Yes, there could be no mistaking that shrewd, jowled face, that curly head. It was Senator Hoey. Swiftly, Wentworth pulled him from the bed, tied a sheet beneath his arms and looped another through it, dragged him toward the open window on the front of the house.

He estimated time swiftly. Had he been too quick in his attack, had Kathleen had time to enter the street? He peered at his watch. Yes, if she moved at exactly the right moment.... Wentworth reached the window and uttered a silent cheer as he saw the limousine gliding to the curb. Kathleen hopped out and Len, on his crutch, was not a moment behind. Wentworth thrust his helpless burden out of the window and lowered him rapidly. Time was so short. Before the others reached this room, he must....

He felt Len Roberts take hold of the limp body, instantly released the improvised rope and whirled back toward the room. His hands flew to pockets inside his coat and dragged out the wig he had prepared in advance. He drew it down over his temples, fitted it securely about the ears and glanced in the mirror. The tousled effect was all right. He was supposed to be sleeping. He tore off coat and shirt and trousers, revealing pajamas beneath them. He kicked off shoes and socks. He thrust rubber pads into the sides of his mouth to distend his jaws, affixed prepared eyebrows. It was hasty, but it should pass.

HE GROPED under the pillow, found a gun, got on slippers

and a bathrobe which was at hand. He fired twice toward the open door, ran to the hallway and raised his voice in a hoarse cry.

"Assassin!" he shouted. "Catch the assassin!" He went to the head of the steps and fired down them twice. He heard the door glass smash and smiled grimly to himself. A man with tousled hair, clad in a bathrobe like himself, came floundering out of another room. He held a gun.

"What's the matter, Senator?"

"I woke up and found a man in my room," Wentworth said in the gruff manner of Hoey. "I shot at him twice and ran out here after him. He jumped through the door, I think. I heard glass break. He killed the guard…" Wentworth turned, paced sharply up and down as Hoey had done on many a lecture platform. "Damn him!" he cried. "Damn him. He tried to kill me." He strode toward his room. "Take care of things, Jukes, and don't let those damned police come in my room. Do y'hear?"

Jukes—Wentworth had recognized the man as Hoey's secretary—muttered an assent and Wentworth closed his door behind him. He went to the bathroom and went swiftly to work upon his face. That momentary appearance had succeeded; now he could perfect the disguise. If Jukes wondered why he had dashed off, he would be told that the excitement had made him a little sick. Hoey was notoriously a physical coward and there would be smiles behind hands, but no questions asked.

When police came, Wentworth interviewed them from his doorway. "You had a narrow escape, Senator Hoey," they assured him. "We don't think there's any doubt it was the same man that attacked you before, the guy who calls himself Corporal Death."

Wentworth braced back his shoulders. "The next time he comes," he said grandiloquently, "I shall wait until he is near enough to make sure of hitting him."

Afterward, Wentworth retired in Senator Hoey's bed. He slept soundly.

He was awake a half hour before a man-servant entered with his breakfast on a tray. Afterwards, contrary to his personal practices, he remained in bed. Hoey always transacted his early morning business in bed, still in pajamas, throwing himself about in absurd attitudes as the boundless energy that drove him stirred within him. Jukes came in.

"I hope you feel all right, sir, after last night's excitement."

Wentworth grunted and reached for the mail. "I want men from all the papers here in half an hour," he said shortly. "An important change of policy to announce."

Jukes bowed, "Yes, sir."

JUKES WENT out smiling. The Senator was a trifle upset by last night's experience. It made Jukes a little sick to see such utter cowardice in a man.

Behind him, Wentworth went rapidly through the mail, but it gave him no hint of the identity of the Mayor of Hell.

Jukes came in and announced the newspaper men. Wentworth looked them over slowly, feeling their hatred, sensing the sneers behind their smiles. He saw that Mitchell, who had been with the *News-Press* and still was with Blake in Newark, had come in with his arm in a sling.

Wentworth threw himself over on his side, holding up his

Wentworth rapidly lowered his helpless burden from the window!

head with a propped elbow, imitating Hoey's abrupt galvanic movements.

"Statement," he said shortly. "I am irrevocably opposed to the financial dictatorship and urge all who may follow my leadership to defeat it at the polls…."

Mitchell took a step forward.

"Senator Hoey, may I ask a question?" he said. "You sponsored this measure. Why is it that…?"

Wentworth scowled at him. "I'll tell you when I get through. Or do you want to get to the telephone now?"

"Yes," said Mitchell. "There'll be an extra on this. It will mean the defeat of the bill if too many haven't voted already…."

WENTWORTH NODDED. "All right. Telephone and get back. There's more and better to come." He flopped flat on his back, spread his legs and cupped his hands beneath his head. When the reporters came back he was pacing the floor barefooted, the smoke of his cigar eddying behind him. He didn't look at them, but began to talk.

"I am taking my life in my hands when I tell you this," he said shortly. "I have been forced to do the things that have been done here in the last month—forced against my will." He stopped and faced them, talking around the cigar, scowling. "I'm a coward. My life has been threatened and men kept near me who would kill me at the least deviation from the orders of the man behind all this. Last night, Corporal Death killed the men who enforced these orders, bless him. I intend to demand general amnesty for that man. Corporal Death is the only hope of the city and the state…."

The newspaper men were taut with the story, ready to dash for telephones. Mitchell gulped loudly.

"Quick, Senator," he urged, "the name of the man who made you do all this."

"He is called," Wentworth said slowly, "the Mayor of Hell. What his real name is, what his face looks like, I do not know. He has only spoken directly to me once, and then it was over the telephone, but from this day on, there's feud between him and me." Wentworth shook a clenched fist over his head. "I'll tell the police everything I know about him and in the end, they'll get him."

The reporters flocked toward the door. Mitchell stepped to the bedside telephone, with an insolent grin at Wentworth. He gave his paper's number, staring sardonically over the instrument into Wentworth's face.

"Anyway, Senator," he said, "if he kills you, you'll be a martyr. They'll probably erect a statue or something."

Wentworth looked over his shoulder toward the door. Everyone had left the room except Mitchell. He dropped the orator's voice of Senator Hoey, said, in his natural tones: "Give that story just as I said it, you louse, and then give my love to Blake."

The phone slipped from Mitchell's hand and when he caught it, he held it crazily, upside down. He stared; then his eyes narrowed. "By God!" he whispered. "By God, I know that voice. It's...."

"Yeah, yeah," he barked into the telephone, then got it right side up. "Yeah, Blake? Listen, Hoey says..." He reeled off the story in staccato sentences. "Yeah, sure it's the truth. I'm in his bedroom right now, looking at him. He'll confirm it, if you want...."

Wentworth growled confirmation into the phone. "And come on back to New York where you can run a decent paper," he said. "You ought to have a million circulation today on that statement of mine."

**BLAKE WAS** shouting his enthusiasm when Wentworth hung up. Mitchell darted for the phone, but Wentworth shook his head.

"Like to stay with me today, young fellow," he growled, "and report the martyrdom of Senator Hoey?"

Mitchell shoved out his hand.

Through the long day, Wentworth transacted the business of Senator Hoey. He demanded general amnesty for Corporal Death, and got it from the state legislature. He cried defiance of the Mayor of Hell, made fresh statements for each edition of the newspapers. He waited hour after hour for the assassins of the Mayor of Hell... and nothing happened.

At ten o'clock that night, when it was certain that the dictatorship was defeated, Wentworth turned to Mitchell and saw that his face was drawn with tension, too. Wentworth smiled slowly.

"We'll beard the lion," he said shortly. "Hunt up the Mayor of Hell?"

Wentworth smiled thinly. "It's a chance, but we'll try it. *Jukes!*"

Jukes popped in at his call.

"Car," Wentworth growled at him. "At once." Jukes tried to insist on a guard but Wentworth sneered at him. "What good would it do? You think ten men would keep the Mayor of Hell out if he wanted to come in?"

Jukes' eyes swung swiftly to Mitchell and he bowed, hiding a smile, Wentworth perceived. That smile puzzled him as he went out into the car. He caught up the speaking tube. "The Big Shot," he growled.

The chauffeur twisted about in his seat, slid back the glass. "You mean… *him*, boss?" he asked anxiously.

"Sure, him." Wentworth agreed.

The chauffeur turned forward reluctantly, slid the glass into place and Wentworth's elbow prodded Mitchell's side. It had worked! They were going to call on the Mayor of Hell! Wentworth's hand went to his coat pocket, clasped delightedly the heavy revolver….

## CHAPTER 20
## MISSING

A S THEY sped toward the stronghold of the Mayor of Hell, Wentworth told Mitchell rapidly about the white room with the glaring light and his conviction that there was another room behind it from which the Mayor of Hell actually operated, by means of a tiny telephone, like a deaf man's instrument, which the dummy man in the white room wore. He recalled the pause before each speech of the man he had killed when he had been taken before the Mayor.

"When I go into the white room," he said. "You must contrive to get into the room behind it and take the man. It's a job I'd like to perform myself, but... Well, I've got to go in from the front."

Twenty minutes after leaving the Senator's home, the car drew up before a Park Avenue apartment house, the chauffeur sprang down and whipped open the door.

"Let me go in with you, Senator," he begged. "I got my rod like always, and...."

Wentworth patted his shoulder. "I'm all right," he said. "I will be all right. Stay here."

He went inside, entered the elevator without a word. If the elevator boy didn't know him, he would be in a spot again. He had no way of telling the apartment number. But the boy didn't say a word, shot him to the twelfth floor and whipped open the door with a bow.

"Here you are, sir."

And they were, too. The foyer was a room such as that other one Wentworth had entered—how long ago?—when he had narrowly escaped with his life and Nita had fallen before a criminal's slug. This room held only one man. He came forward uncertainly.

"Geez," he said. "You certainly played hell today. I'm the only one stuck around, except *him.*" He jerked his head toward the door that Wentworth guessed hid the white room. "All the boys figured it was the pay-off and took it on the lam."

Wentworth turned to Mitchell. "Wait here." He faced the crook. "Come with me." He went straight toward the door of the white room and the crook danced ahead and slid it back.

"Geez, Senator," he whined. "You oughter appreciate me

sticking around like this when I could of took a powder when the rest of them did."

"I do appreciate it," Wentworth assured him gravely.

He walked into the white room and the lights blazed out. "Turn out that damned thing," he snapped and the light died, except for small ones that showed him the scare-crow figure at the end of the room. The man was gaunt and long and his face was made up, Wentworth saw, so that it was dead white with black rings about the eyes. It took no second look to know that this was not the man he sought.

"Well, *you* stuck around anyway," Wentworth said.

The man shrugged, said in a deep, actor's voice, "What else was there for me to do? I had no place in that crowd of crooks. My masquerade was not actually anything criminal despite the things I've been forced to do. I'm glad now that it's all over. My pay has been most liberal." The man bowed gracefully.

Wentworth frowned. There was something elusive in the atmosphere, like Jukes' smile, that he could not quite understand. He had expected to spread dissension among the ranks of the Mayor of Hell, but this victory was positively overwhelming. He walked past the actor and, looking down at the floor, saw the fine wires through which the Mayor of Hell spoke to his mouth-pieces.

"Let me have the gadget," he said.

HE WAS realizing that the room beyond must be empty. Either that, or these two men were maneuvering him into position for an easy kill. These men acted almost as if... With a sudden oath he took the phone device which was, as he had guessed, the type used by deaf people, a tiny, bean-like receiver which fitted into the ear. He put it in his, and immediately a voice spoke to him.

"It's the pay-off, Corporal Death. There's no Mayor of Hell or anything else in here." It was Mitchell speaking.

Wentworth nodded shortly. His eyes were blazing. He whirled on the two men. "You two clear out. You'll hear from me later." He strode sharply toward the door and Mitchell came out of another entrance, strolled toward him.

"Going, Senator?" he asked.

"Yes."

Wentworth did not speak while he drifted downward in the elevator, nor afterward when he entered the waiting limousine, but twice he looked into the rear-vision mirror attached in his own compartment and saw that another sedan followed. Excitement was singing through his veins. If what he suspected....

He turned to Mitchell. "Describe the room you were in," he ordered.

Mitchell shook his head. "It wasn't a room, it was a closet. There was a big chair. Drinks and cigars." He pulled a smoke from his pocket and offered it. "Good ones, too. There was a piece of silvery looking-glass that I could see right through, and I could hear everything said in the white room. There was a microphone there, too, that I could talk through."

Wentworth took the cigar the reporter offered, drew it under his nostrils. He smiled slowly. The expression would not have been pleasant on Wentworth's normal face. On that of Senator

Hoey, it was singularly sinister. He leaned forward and tapped on the glass, and the chauffeur drew to the curb.

"Go back to the Senator's house, and wait for me there," Wentworth told Mitchell. "I'm going to have a chat with the Mayor of Hell."

Mitchell stared at him, wide-eyed. "Hey! Who is he? How do you know where to find him?"

Wentworth opened the door of the car, delayed to speak to the chauffeur. "Take this gentleman to the house," he said. "Tell Jukes he is to give him some of my cigars."

He closed the door and the limousine pulled off. Wentworth walked slowly back along the pavement, signaled the black sedan which had been following him. Kathleen was behind the wheel, dark circles under her young eyes. For a moment she hesitated, glanced into the back of the car, then slowed to the curb. She stared at him directly, unswervingly, but there was no relaxation in her guard.

Wentworth smiled. His disguise must be very good indeed. "Thank you, Kathleen," he said in his normal voice. "You have done an excellent job."

The girl smiled widely. "Oh, thank God!" she said. "I couldn't tell... I wasn't sure...."

Wentworth nodded, opened the back door of the car and got in. Senator Hoey was clad a little more warmly than when Wentworth had last seen him. He had on an overcoat that O'Rourke had given him and there was a robe wrapped around his knees. When he saw Wentworth his eyes narrowed.

"So that was the idea of the kidnapping, was it?" he sneered in his bullying, deep voice. "When are you going to quit playing around and let me go?"

"Right now, Senator Hoey," Wentworth said pleasantly, "or at least as soon as I give you some clothing. Kathleen, will you take us to your hotel? Think you can drive us from there, Pat?" PAT O'ROURKE'S face was drained with weariness. But the smile widened slowly on his thick, solid lips.

"Sure, I can drive from now until the O'Rourke banshee screams," he said, "now that you're back with us again."

Kathleen alighted from the driver's seat and Pat O'Rourke took her place. Kathleen leaned in at the door, her eyes going anxiously from the face of the man she loved to that of Wentworth.

"When," her voice broke, "when will I see you again?"

"You'll see Len within an hour," Wentworth said.

Kathleen closed the door and Pat O'Rourke sent the car rolling forward. Wentworth looked back and Kathleen still stood in front of the hotel, looking after them, her hands clasped before her. Abruptly, she flung up a hand in a childlike wave, and ran into the hotel.

Senator Hoey sneered. "Very touching. I suppose you're Corporal Death?"

"Quite," Wentworth murmured. "I trust you have seen the day's papers? Your dictatorship was defeated."

Hoey nodded slowly with a stoicism no man could have expected. "Quite," he mimicked. "Do you think you can get away with it? Wait until the Mayor of Hell gets busy...."

"He won't, again, Senator Hoey." Wentworth nodded. "Have

a cigar, won't you, Senator?" he handed him the one that had come from the chair in which the Mayor of Hell had sat. Hoey reached for it hungrily.

"By God," he grunted, "I've been wanting one for hours and these mugs…" He sniffed at it, bit off an end, and tucked it between his teeth, inhaled deeply while Wentworth held a match. "One of my own, too! I pay ninety-four cents apiece for them wholesale, but they're worth it." He sucked smoke deep.

Wentworth turned to Len Roberts. "You heard what he said, Len?" he asked.

Roberts nodded. "You mean about how much the cigars cost?"

"About that being one of his own."

Roberts nodded and Hoey's face paled. He took the cigar from his mouth, staring.

"That cigar which he admits is his, Roberts," Wentworth said softly, "came from an apartment on Park Avenue…."

"This isn't my cigar," Hoey said sharply. "I thought it was, but it isn't…."

"In that apartment, Roberts, was a white room such as we found in that place on Central Park, West, remember?"

"Sure, where the Mayor of Hell had a dummy to speak for him, I remember."

"It isn't my cigar!" Hoey cringed back on the cushions. "I swear it isn't."

"Yes," said Wentworth. "Well, in the closet behind the dummy, was a very comfortable chair from which the Mayor of Hell spoke…."

"I gave him those cigars!" whined Hoey. "I admit I worked with him. I gave him those cigars."

"You mean," Roberts was leaning forward, "this cigar was in a box by the chair?"

"Yes," Wentworth said. "Pat, will you stop at that corner drug store? I want to make a telephone call. Roberts, if he opens his mouth, shove your gun down his throat."

WENTWORTH WENT to the corner drug store and made a telephone call and came back. He pulled down the car shades and began to strip off Hoey's clothes, which he wore, donned others from a suitcase on the floor of the car. He handed the senator his own suit.

"Get dressed," he ordered brusquely.

Senator Hoey scrambled into the clothing eagerly, a strained, pleading look on his face. He kept his eyes on Wentworth as he stripped off the wig and the bits of disguise from his face.

"What did you find out?" Roberts asked grimly.

"I telephoned Mitchell, a newspaper man I sent to Hoey's house," Wentworth replied gravely. "At my request, he searched the closet in Hoey's bedroom, and found that it was fitted up like that one on Park Avenue and that there was a white room beyond the partition in the wall, just as there was on Park Avenue. I think that proves my point, Hoey, that *you are the Mayor of Hell!*"

A snarl like the rage of an animal rasped from Hoey's jaws. His hand whipped from beneath the coat he was donning and leveled a revolver at Wentworth's breast, Wentworth's own revolver, left in the pockets.

"Yes, I'm the Mayor of Hell," Hoey said, "You were a bit too confident, Mr. Corporal Death. And you were careless. You left a gun in the pocket of your coat. You die, now, and tomorrow, I'll be in power again. I can kill Kirkpatrick easily. Coddington, too, if it's worth while." Senator Hoey threw back his head and laughed heartily. "To think that Corporal Death would make such a mistake as leaving his revolver in clothes he handed to a prisoner…. Now… *you die…!*"

Wentworth's left hand became a blur as it jolted the Senator's gun upward. Even so, the bullet seared his cheek, made the entire side of his face numb. Wentworth's right hand came out of his coat pocket and he began pulling the trigger. He emptied the chambers of his revolver.

"Drive ahead, Pat," he ordered calmly, scarcely able to hear his voice with the thunder of his shots still in them. He turned to Roberts. "We'll leave the body in the car and the city will say that the Mayor of Hell found him at last. They will build statues to their martyred senator."

"Hell," said Roberts, "Hell, you… shot him wide open…."

Wentworth looked on the corpse without emotion…. "Today Hoey gained amnesty for Corporal Death—and for his helpers, Len Roberts, Pat and Kathleen O'Rourke. For myself, I would never have done that, but I promised Kathleen that you should be cleared."

The car screeched around corners, then slowed, as Pat O'Rourke sought a dark street. Wentworth leaned back heavily on the cushions. He was weary, terribly weary. For him, the fight was not yet over. He still must clear up the charges that Commissioner Fogarty had brought against Richard Wentworth. Until he did that, Jackson and Ram Singh could not be freed from prison; he could not be seen openly with Nita and each visit he paid her would be putting his head into the noose of the law and endangering her. Moreover, the flight of the gunmen of the Mayor of Hell did not end the reign of crime and corrupt politics that held the city. Tomorrow, if he went to Kirkpatrick in his own identity, Kirkpatrick would order his arrest on Fogarty's charges. It was Kirkpatrick's utter integrity, his unswerving devotion to duty that made him valuable in his position—his willingness to sacrifice everything he held dear upon the altar of duty. So Wentworth was barred from help there. But he could rest a little while now, with the Mayor of Hell terribly dead, with the political power of Hoey shattered.

"This is all right, Pat," he called. The car slowed to a halt and Wentworth got out. He shivered a little in the direct blast of the wind from the River. It was not very late, not yet midnight. He could put his head into the noose of the law tonight, could go to kneel once more by Nita's bedside. He smiled faintly.

"All right, boys, let's go."

Roberts swung along on his crutches. Pat O'Rourke moved heavily, with the weakness of a man who has been long ill. They were drained of strength, now that the battle was over.

"I say, Corporal Death," Roberts said finally, "it was damned careless—leaving your gun in that coat pocket. He might have killed you."

Wentworth laughed shortly. "No, Len," he said, "not careless, very careful. I never have been able to kill a man in cold blood."